Copyright © 2022 by Mark Matoc

All rights reserved.

The characters and events portrayed in this book are fictitious. Any similarity to real persons, living or dead, is coincidental and not intended by the author.

No part of this book may be reproduced, or stored in a retrieval system, or transmitted in any form or by any means, electronic, mechanical, photocopying, recording, or otherwise, without express written permission of the author.

The following selections were previously published: "Stay With Me" in *Spine* magazine, "The People in 2B" in *Lunatics* magazine; "zombie. com" in *Parasite Gods*; "Yours Truly" in *Devil's Rejects*; "Every Hunt Is A Cold One" in *Bitter Chills*.

Excerpts from "The Strange Case of Dr. Jekyll and Mr. Hyde" by Robert Louis Stevenson, "Fire and Ice" by Robert Frost, and "The Revolt of the Angels" by Anatole France used under the terms of Public Domain.

ISBN: 978-1-7773486-3-2

Cover art by Mitch Green.

PRAISE FOR MARCUS HAWKE AND THE MIRACLE SIN

"A rollercoaster of horror and tension."

— MICHAEL BENAVIDEZ, AUTHOR OF *WHEN ANGELS FAIL: AS THE SHADOWS GROW*

"This book does not hold back, it does not shy away from the nitty-gritty, and certainly keeps you coming back for more."

— SABRINA VOERMAN, AUTHOR OF *RED*

"A tragic, grueling journey of self-reflection, with beloved characters who now hold a special place in my heart. Mason is a relatable MC, and I felt like a part of the story as I joined him in his endeavors. Marcus is one incredible writer. His attention to detail is something to be admired, and I thoroughly enjoyed the flow, structure, and pace of *The Miracle Sin*. Profound themes, charming characters, and a lot of great laughs await you! One of my favorite reads of 2021."

— SHANNON LANE, AUTHOR OF *SOUL ON FIRE*

"I can't say enough for this masterwork. It's clever and funny as hell while being torturously terrifying."

— CALEB RYAN, @THE_BOOKEYMAN

"Marcus does great work in this book, he has an eye for character and writes with wit and elegant style. He can brutal yet tender at once. I can't wait to read what he does next."

— JAMIE STEWART, AUTHOR OF *THE HOUSE THAT BLEEDS*

"This is exactly the kind of story that I live for; something deep enough to get lost in, a world created and unveiled for me to explore, to find wonder and horror alike. A story that makes me think, makes me ask questions and makes me wonder at what else this world may hold."

— CANDACE NOLA, AUTHOR OF *BREACH*

"As I sit here trying to write this review, I am finding myself to be at a loss for words. That is something that rarely happens…I found this to be absolutely wonderful in every way possible. The prose is stunning, the characters are well developed, and the themes are a medley, filled with some brutal moments, and yet there is a tenderness that is heartfelt. Religious undertones that makes the mind question, loss of human life, human suffering and questioning faith…I just love the depth of this and it has nestled itself into my soul."

— KARLA PETERSON, AMAZON REVIEW

"The Miracle Sin is unique and I never knew which direction it would take. At times, horror -- other times comedy, other times a thriller...It is hard to describe it in detail since it is so vast and broad. I will simply say that reading this will not disappoint! Something for everyone!"

— BILLY RAY MIDDLETON JR., AUTHOR OF *THE NICEST PARTS OF HELL*

"Admittedly I'm not the biggest thriller/horror fan so I went into this a little unsure. However, Marcus reminded me that it's not just the story but how you tell it and he did a phenomenal job telling Mason's! Several times I caught myself rereading a line because I was so impressed with how well written it was."

— BEE DAVIS, AMAZON REVIEW

"The book has quite the action in it with just the right amount of blood and guts. There we're definitely a few scenes that had me clutching my pearls and going for my smelling salts."

— GRACE REYNOLDS, AUTHOR OF *LADY OF THE HOUSE*

These stories, while fictional, contain many real world horrors such as violence, abuse, torture, self-harm, suicide, grief, incest, implied harm to minors, trauma, and murder, in addition to other mature content.

Reader discretion is advised.

CONTENTS

Preface	xi
The People in 2B	1
zombie.com	15
Just One of Those Things	32
Stay With Me	49
Doll	54
Under the Black Top	66
Slasher	87
School Spirit	99
Yours Truly	108
Every Hunt is a Cold One	121
Matters of the Heart	138
The Reign and The Rapture	150
Chapter One	177
About the Author	183
Also by Marcus Hawke	185

PREFACE

Each of these stories has a purpose. Or at least they did at one point. More often than not, that purpose was, as you might safely guess, to tell a story. Others because an idea occurred to me, one I couldn't forget and had to get out. A few because there was a submission call to which the story was catered. But what I didn't expect was that regardless of what seeded them, each of them would wind up being therapeutic.

Very few did I set out to exercise any one particular demon, it just sort worked out that way. Instead it was more akin to someone asking a person how they are, and before the dot can be put on the question mark, they're giving you their full dirty laundry list of woes. So in order to give you some background of what served as mortar for these existential bricks, I've attached some commentary to the end of each one.

I offer my deepest gratitude to my editors, Cara Flannery and Matthew Day, for making these perverse offerings readable; as well as to the editors of the publications in which some of them first appeared. Thank you to Mitch Green for creating artwork so wonderfully grotesque that it caught my eye and even partially influenced one of the stories. And last but most, to my Tabby

PREFACE

who read each and every one of these before being submitted, after they were published, the ones that weren't accepted, and the ones written exclusively for this collection. Additionally, for being there for me through many of the tribulations for which these stories are the result.

And of course to you, dear reader. May God have mercy on your soul.

-MH-

July 22, 2022

"With every day, and from both sides of my intelligence, the moral and the intellectual, I thus drew steadily nearer to the truth, by whose partial discovery I have been doomed to such a dreadful shipwreck: that man is not truly one, but truly two."

— *THE STRANGE CASE OF DR. JEKYLL AND MR. HYDE*, ROBERT LOUIS STEVENSON

THE PEOPLE IN 2B

My name is Bob Bradley. I am writing this now while I have a minute so my side of the story is heard and not lost or distorted in the news. For almost a year now, I have lived at 220 Fenwick Street, Apartment 2A. Not a big place—one bedroom, one and a half baths, with a living room, kitchenette with a little breakfast nook I've been using to grade papers. The building itself isn't very big either. There are only six floors, two apartments per floor.

In a perfect world, it would be the right fit for a nineteen-year-old kid who just moved out from home for the first time. But the world is definitely not perfect, and the reality is that it was the only place I could afford after my divorce. And barely at that.

From the day I moved in, I've been plagued by the relentless noise coming from the apartment across the hall: 2B.

Or not 2B. HA!

Now to be fair, it's partially due to the fact that this is an older building and there's little insulation between apartments to speak of. Suitable or not, if I was a model tenant, the people in 2B would be just the opposite. The type nobody likes living near.

Not one day has passed that I haven't been able to hear the deafening ruckus of what must be surround-sound speakers the size of refrigerators as they watch television. The couple who live there fight late at night, waking me up in the process. And their child—oh God, that child—screams and cries and raises holy hell any time he doesn't get what he wants. I should know. As I said, the walls are so thin that it sounds as if the commotion is coming from the next room rather than next door.

The worst part is that when I viewed the apartment, there wasn't a peep to be heard let alone shouting at volumes usually reserved for victims of a burning car.

I gave them the benefit of the doubt at first, foolishly hoping this was something that was not constant. It didn't take long for me to realize just how wrong I was.

One day I bumped into the family as I was getting off the elevator on my way to work. He was a tall, well-built man perhaps in his early thirties. His wife, a little bit younger, attractive but distant. And their son was a towheaded boy who reminded me of my son Ian at that age.

I introduced myself, made niceties. The young man introduced himself as Neil, his wife as Michelle.

"And this little guy is our son, Jagger," said Neil, tousling the hair of the boy next to him, whose face was buried in some video game device.

I remember having to fight not to roll my eyes at the names parents give their children these days, but I wasn't going to let it ruin things when they were going well.

The little whelp! I could smell it in him. Trouble and nothing but!

"Nice to meet you," I said a little too impatiently. I'm not sure why I was nervous, but confrontation has never been my strong suit. They began to head for the elevator when I spoke up. "Actually, I was wondering if I might have a word with you."

Neil stopped, cocked his head and narrowed his eyes as if straining to think of what could possibly be the matter.

I mentioned the noise, the late-night screaming matches and the fact that their "little guy" was the last thing I needed to hear after a long day at work to pay for my ex-wife's alimony (though I didn't put it quite that way).

Once I had finished, Neil just stared at me with his arms crossed. He did not look impressed.

"Well, if you've got a problem you can take it up with the super," he said sharply. Neil turned his back on me and joined his wife and son.

No compassion. No apology. Nothing.

"I'd rather not have to get the building management involved, but if that's what you want," I said, clinging to my composure. It was an empty threat, but I tried not to flinch, not to let it show.

"Whatever, gramps," he replied with an uncaring shrug.

Stunned, I caught one last thing before the elevator doors shut —his son looking up from his video game just long enough to stick his tongue out at me.

I have never been so angry or insulted in my life! I was livid with rage and disgust and wanted to march straight to their apartment, bang on the door and give him the fat lip he deserved.

But I didn't.

Instead I did the only thing I could: called my therapist.

She helped calm me down, but it was a living hell. Powerless and outraged without a single drop of booze. Dr. Byrne knew my situation, knew I was recently divorced and said like it or not, this apartment was my home; somewhere I should feel comfortable and safe. Her words would have helped more if they weren't spoiled by the boom of speakers so loud my dishes rattled.

Dr. Byrne suggested that I do what my neighbor mockingly suggested and call the superintendent, but she was sure to remind me that no matter what happens, alcohol doesn't solve problems, it creates them. I knew she was right. It wasn't worth throwing away five months of sobriety.

So I did just that.

The building manager, a man by the name of Trevor, sounded like he had recently undergone a lobotomy. It was amazing just how obvious this man's desire to get me off the phone was. He assured me that he would handle it and hung up, leaving me certain that nothing would be done.

Mr. Gellar in 1B said it sounded like a family of drunken elephants lived above him. Mrs. Moseby said her floor often shook. Even the younger girl with the lip piercing who lives just beneath me agreed. I mentioned that I had called the building manager to complain and got the same response from all: "Good luck."

I see now how naïve that was. Did I really think that no one had complained before, that no one had tried and failed? How many futile attempts at getting the police to do something had occurred? How long had the woman who formerly lived in my apartment fought before finally giving up and moving out?

The next several months went unchanged. I'd see Neil or his wife in the hall, or the elevator, and each time the tension was palpable. It hung thick in the air, like gunslingers sizing each other up just before high noon.

Of course the riot next door continued. I attempted to drown it out by turning the volume on my own television up when I watched it, which was not very often. Unfortunately, this was fighting fire with cotton balls. There was little I could do when I wanted to quietly read the newspaper.

I started to get headaches from not just the noise but the frustration as well. The stress even gave me a nosebleed or two. Eventually, I began to notice a splinter in my mind, a schism that over time grew as the presence of peace and quiet vanished. I know now that it was madness overcoming, blooming in me like a bloodstain in soiled gauze. It became a voice. An honest-to-God voice, separate from my own, had appeared in my brain. It didn't sound like mine at all, but I had heard this voice before. Soft and comforting, almost feminine in the way it coaxed me to listen. And when I did, it told me terrible things.

It told me the people next door were making fun of me.

Mocking me.

Laughing at me.

You know they are! You know it!

He said they could do as they pleased and I was weak and powerless to stop them. They could do as they pleased because Neil's brother-in-law was the building manager. He also told me that their little brat wasn't even his. He was the result of Neil's best friend screwing his wife's brains out while he was engaging in his own debauchery at a bachelor party in Las Vegas. He had no clue, not the slightest inkling that his son wasn't his at all.

And she loved it! Secretly it was her reason for living, silently enjoying the fact that he thought he was "the Man," King of the Castle, bringing home the bacon for Momma and Baby Bear. She loved the fact that he wore the pants in the family while someone else was getting in hers. It was what she thought of when they made love, short-lived though it was since he was never between her legs for more than sixty seconds.

I mentioned this to Dr. Byrne during my next session. She asked from where I thought the voice came. As soon as she did, I knew right away that it was Lefty, my imaginary friend from childhood.

When I was a boy, he looked exactly like me, only he was a mirror image. He even wrote with his left hand while I was right-handed. He helped me do the things I was too scared to do, helped me stand up to my fifth grade bully, Chad Dexter. Sometimes, though, he wanted to do things like sneak into the girl's changing room or start a fire just for fun. I never gave in because I knew it was wrong.

To me, he never felt imaginary. Even after I grew out of him, it felt as if he was never far, watching behind my eyes, resting just beneath my tongue.

When I told Dr. Byrne about him (leaving the more mischievous parts out), she encouraged me to get in touch with him again. I think she meant it as an attempt to reconnect with my inner child or whatever it is therapists think.

I started by writing him a letter as if he were an old pen pal. When I was done, I somehow found the pen in my left hand, writing his name across the bottom of the page. Then there he was, standing behind me. He had aged just as I had, with a full beard, wrinkles, spare tire, greying hair. Everything the same.

It started small. I would talk to him about Helen and the boys and how my drinking problem had driven them all away. He said it was okay that my ex was a cold, heartless bitch and that my own sons didn't even offer to help me move.

"Because I'm here for you now, Bobby," he told me.

I'm back...and this time I ain't goin' nowhere!

No one had called me Bobby in a very long time. Whenever Helen wanted my attention she called me Robert. It drove me nuts.

Lefty began showing up more and more, suggesting we go for a walk in the evenings or take in a movie. "Sure, even on a school night," he'd say. "Anything to get away from that racket!"

He even showed up while I was teaching a class once or twice. There he'd be, sitting in an empty desk near the back when my students were practically asleep.

Lefty didn't like my boss, Principal Miller, and said I should choke him with the god-awful paisley neckties he wore, or that I should wait until he and I are standing shoulder to shoulder at the urinal, and at the right moment, turn and piss all over him. I have to admit, that made me laugh.

Clearly I was completely losing my mind, I see that now. But at the time, it all seemed very normal, like getting reacquainted with an old friend. For a while, that's just how it went.

Eventually it grew colder, our outings less frequent and finally winter arrived, along with the claustrophobia and isolation that comes with it. Just getting from Point A to Point B in winter weather was miserable enough without trying to come up with extra reasons to suffer through it. This gave Lefty and I little choice but to be cooped up inside and that goddamn noise just would not stop!

In fact, it got worse. I watched them through my peephole as the holiday season brought the inevitable comings and goings of friends and family dropping off gifts and plates of gingerbread men. I wouldn't have minded so much, except that they were all as obnoxious as their hosts. When New Year's Eve came, guess who hosted the bash? You better believe it.

Lefty said I should go across the hall and start banging on the door, shout, curse, throw eggs at their door, ride a tricycle naked through the hall singing "Frosty the Snowman." Something. Anything!

Show 'em you got claws of your own, Bobby Boy, and they'll think twice. Oh they'll think then, and regret it, and beg and it'll be too late. Not so merry now, are we?

I couldn't. It just wasn't in me.

Not yet...

All I could hear when I closed my eyes was noise. NOISE,

NOISE, NOISE! My whole world had been penetrated, invaded by it. I heard it when I went to sleep, even when there was none. The instant I heard a child cry in public, my pulse spiked. I'd bite my nails, clench my teeth and try to get the hell away from wherever I was. I heard it in class and shouted at students that had not made a peep.

It seemed that there truly was no escape.

I suppose I had better wrap this up while I'm still a free man.

Last week I was doing my laundry. The laundry room is on the bottom floor and I don't see the sense in taking the elevator when the stairwell is...I may as well be honest: I all but stopped taking the elevator. There it is. I decided it just wasn't worth the displeasure of bumping into THEM. Plus it's only one floor really, and I didn't mind walking.

So I took the stairs, and right away could hear the sound of a little siren. I could feel my chest tighten even as I reached the last set of steps before the bottom floor, and sure enough, there was Jagger. Here was a boy of no more than five-years-old, unsupervised, playing with a toy truck on the landing of a stairwell. I mean, what kind of parents allow this to happen?

Despite the whispering in my brain, I was resolved to just mind my business.

He didn't even seem to notice me until I towered over him with my laundry hamper. He didn't move, just stared at me blankly as if trying to figure out whether I was human or not.

I forced a smile. "Excuse me."

No response.

"I said excuse me, son."

Again, nothing. His blue little eyes frozen like a mannequin.

The smile disappeared and I put down the hamper. "I need to get by. Can you move, please?"

I just meant to move him out of the way, that's all. I just

needed him off the stairs for five seconds so I could pass. As soon as I made a motion toward him, the little bastard started to scream at the top of his lungs! I didn't even touch him. He just kept shrieking over and over and over like a stuck pig and all I can remember was thinking STOP! STOP! STOP!

The next thing I knew I was standing above him, but he was not in front of me.

He was at the bottom of the stairs.

That image is burned in my brain—his slumped body resting on the last step, blonde little head facing the other way when it should have been facing the floor. My shadow stretched over him, broken on the angles of the steps.

I don't know what happened, but I have a pretty good idea. Somehow, I thought, I must have snapped, like bad wiring glued poorly in place that had finally come loose. Instead of a memory, there was a big black void.

I remember thinking that I was going to be caught red-handed that very moment, standing there, unable to move. I could almost picture his grief-stricken mother's face poking around the doorway to the laundry room. She'd been in there all along, right? Of course. She had to be. No mother could just leave her son alone like that...

But nothing happened. I tell you, no one came. I couldn't believe it, but it was true. Everyone must have been so used to living with the noise he and his parents made, why would anyone come? For all I knew she was passed out from one too many afternoon glasses of Chardonnay.

Slowly, I turned and went back up the stairs, quietly at first, one step at a time. I stopped dead in my tracks and very nearly tripped when I rushed back for my hamper. Once I had it, I flew up the steps and clumsily through my door.

I collapsed to the floor, my back against the wall, hugging my knees and rocking back and forth. My eyes were fixed on the wall where a Home, Sweet Home sign hung. It was one of the few things I got to keep from my old house, the only other being a Number One Dad trophy my boys gave me one year for Father's Day on a nearby shelf.

After what seemed like hours, the shock disappeared and panic set in as I heard the fumbling of keys at the door. Alert and stiff with fright, I realized it was Neil returning home from work.

I could hear some muttering going on after he entered his apartment, but couldn't quite make out what was said, only the names of his wife and son. Then there was a sudden flurry of movement before the door flew open with a loud crack as it slammed against the wall.

Mother and Father were calling their child's name, worried, terrified at the thoughts that would surely be racing through any parent's head.

"Where could he be?"

"I DON'T KNOW!"

They split up. Papa took the elevator as Mama went through the stairwell door. Then finally the moment came, and a blood-curdling scream exploded up through the stairwell like a banshee on fire.

I felt Lefty's hand on my shoulder and heard his greasy voice in my head.

Bravo, Bobby.

"I'm fucked, Lefty. It's only a matter of time before—"

Before what, you big silly? When someone's found at the foot of the stairs, no one thinks of murder.

"You did this, didn't you!" I said.

Of course. You're welcome!

I couldn't see him, but I felt his crooked grin curling against my own lips. I recoiled in horror, and after vomiting on my own feet, my mantra resumed.

"What have I done? What have I done?"

How long I stayed like that, I can't say. All I know is that at some point the police and EMS arrived, at which point a crowd had gathered outside the building. Some tenants, some passersby.

Sickening how if someone were screaming for help, strangers would ignore it and carry on, but all it takes to draw their attention is the mere sight of an ambulance.

Whether out of common sense or Lefty's suggestion, I'm not sure, but I too eventually joined the solemn little crowd. I gasped and shook my head as they did, pretending to have no knowledge of the events. Some provided secondhand accounts of what they heard and why they didn't act sooner.

That was when I realized just how easy it was. Almost too easy. And when I took care of the boy's parents, that was easy as apple pie.

They had just returned home from the funeral and began fighting almost immediately. Neil was screaming at Michelle, telling her it was all her fault. She started banging on the wall, crying the same mournful wail I heard when she discovered her son's body.

She began throwing things, and as the glass shattered against our poor excuse for a wall, the tremors in my brain returned again. Every crash of glass felt like a crooked nail hammered into my skull. I too began to shout and scratch at my face, finally collapsing to the floor.

I looked up, saw the trophy. Number One Dad.

Blackness again.

Lefty took over.

When it was finished, I stood overlooking their lifeless bodies, the base of my trophy clutched tightly. Odd how this small white thing would normally seem no more harmful than a cup of tea, but it was now covered in blood and cutting into the skin of my hand from the ruthless grip.

There were bits I remembered after. A jaunty little knock on the door

Howdy, neighbor!

followed by pounding over the angry words, the gush of blood, cries and gasps and Lefty laughing. Broken bits of gold plastic stuck out from the cuts in Neil's face, Michelle's with one eye closed, the other half open like the moon hidden behind a wisp of cloud.

I'd done it again...and this time, I liked it.

Darkness crept in and I began to know real terror. Only this time there was no lapse in memory. Quite the opposite. I went to the bathroom mirror and saw Lefty. No longer was my reflection cast back at me, but rather a wretch of twisted teeth in the most loveless smile I'd ever seen. The skin was black and seemed to breathe like each limb held a pair of lungs. The eyes were black too, rimmed in yellow-white like twin suns in eclipse. When their cruel light met my gaze, I was lost to a nightmare. This was the time of bad things. Every horror, every unspeakable act that darts across one's mind throughout life now revived and incarnate. Screams at the acts I committed. Cries at perversions I dare not speak of even here. I tasted blood. Tore flesh. All traces of humanity burned away in the brimstone of my mind. I gave in fully to the thing, the fiend I had become.

And all the while Lefty hissed in horrid climax:

Yes! Yes!!! YESSSSSSSS!!!!!!

I will be caught eventually, of course. It's only a matter of time before a friend or family member stops by, having not heard from them in several days. One of the neighbors may have already heard the screams, and this time they may call the police. They may be on their way right now. Then again, maybe not.

Whatever the case, I sit at my kitchen table, savoring the precious silence I've needed for so long...but even now, even though they're all gone, I can still hear that little brat screaming and crying, screaming and crying, screaming and crying...

DEAR GOD! PLEASE MAKE IT STOP!!!

In closing, I just want to say that I'm not a bad person. Not really. Everyone at some point in life has had neighbors like mine. If you're reading this letter, chances are you know just what I'm talking about. You've thought it yourself. You may not admit it, but everyone's dreamt of getting even. Sweet revenge. Throttling them, wanting to beat them to a pulp just to get some peace of mind, promising yourself that the next time they disturb you, you'll do something about it once and for all. The only difference between us is that I made good on my promise.

Sincerely,
    Robert Bradley

Lefty

P.S. They say it's the quiet ones you've got to watch out for. I guess they were right.

I've lived in the same building for twelve years and in that time I've dealt with everything from noise, to property destruction, fist fights, drug dealing, squatters, two consecutive infestations of bed bugs, unsupervised children using stairwells as playgrounds, drunken karaoke jams, boisterous arguments at 2 AM, actual honest-to-god dumpster fires, breaking and entering, coyotes (yes, really), water damage from burst pipes, and homeless gaining entry because the outer doors were left propped open by other residents. All in a building where you can hear the toilets flush, the walls are so thin. But only one shooting…so far.

If you haven't experienced this level of fuckery, there's little I can say that will convey how dark, and dreary, and maddening, and in all other ways scary a thing it is. If you have experienced it, I'm sure I don't have to.

ZOMBIE.COM

THE CLEAR BLUE WATER OF THE MEDITERRANEAN HELD Malcolm's gaze as deeply as a swaying pendulum. Not a soul around for miles. On the horizon, the white edge of a sailboat could be seen, frozen in time and space between the sea and the sky. The waves gently lapped against the shore and he could almost feel the slightest breeze.

Almost.

The shrill ring of his phone broke the spell, paradise reverting back to the same creased, faded postcard that had been stuck to his computer monitor for the last four years. Malcolm recognized the extension on the display immediately. It was the same one he saw at least twelve times a day, each time hitting him with a familiar knot of nausea.

He let out a long sigh and picked up the receiver mid-ring. "Yes, Mister Bolton?"

"Mister Moore," came the high, whiny voice from the other end. "You were supposed to be in my office nine minutes ago for your performance review."

Malcolm cringed at the inflection of his boss's voice, simultaneously reminding and scolding him. He looked at the time in the bottom right corner of his computer screen. It was nearly ten minutes after eleven.

"Sorry, sir. I was just…"

"…Yes?"

Oh god… what? Just what? Sending a fax? On a call with a client? Taking a leak? Malcolm fumbled for some feeble excuse but the shores of Ibiza were still swirling in his mind like the last dregs of cold coffee in an empty pot.

"That's alright," said Mr. Bolton, pleasant as could be. "You can just subtract it from your lunch hour."

Prick, said Malcolm inside his head, while aloud he assured his boss that he'd be right there. He hung up the phone and got up to leave when he heard the tiny blip of a new e-mail.

The sender line read: gromero@zombie.com

RE: BRAINS!!!

It looked like either junk or one of the many goofy e-mails that circulated around the office. Dogs playing poker, subtitled "Staff Meeting" or "Wanted: A Raise, Last Seen: My Boss's Office." Each one eliciting phony laughs from some, painful eye rolls from others.

Malcolm hit the delete key and left his cubicle.

"Hey, Malcolm," said Zack, the office clown, as he stepped into the elevator Malcolm had just exited. "How's life in the Hole?" The elevator door closed in just enough time for Malcolm to catch a smug, shit-eating grin.

The floor was abuzz with people going on about their day. Pecking away at keyboards, getting coffee, sending faxes. The usual. It had the sterile smell of a hospital. Everyone seemed to speak with the dreamy countenance of psych ward patients high on Thorazine. The cubicle configuration formed little pathways that zigzagged across the floor like a giant ant farm. Right there in the middle was an empty one. His.

Malcolm made his way down the aisle and to the door on the right. Stan Bolton's office. His secretary, Betty, sat at her desk across from it while she filed her polished nails. With her black bouffant hair, eyelashes too long to be real and red lipstick matching the dress that hugged her plump body, she looked like a chubby ladybug with cleavage. She gave Malcolm a little wink as he approached.

Pencil thin, with glasses and a bushy moustache on his long face, Mr. Bolton was scribbling away on a pad of paper behind an enormous oak desk that took up most of the room. He reminded Malcolm of his high school principal, Mr. Snodgrass, and like Mr. Snodgrass, they both wore the same cheap gold watch, a gift no doubt given to mark their tenure of however many years it took to acquire such a thing. But what Malcolm found the most ridiculous about this man was what had to be the worst hairpiece he had ever seen in his life.

The office itself was plain. No pictures, not a stitch of additional or unnecessary furniture, almost nothing to indicate that he existed outside the hours of 9 a.m. to 5 p.m. A green lamp on the desk and the leather chair in which he sat were the only things that stood out at all.

Malcolm knocked softly on the open door.

"Ah, Mister Moore," said Mr. Bolton in his nasal voice as he looked up from the desk. "Please, come in." Malcolm closed the door behind him and took a seat. "How are you today?"

Living the dream, Stan. Thanks for asking. He put on a smile, forced his best happy worker façade, and issued a surprisingly cheery, "Good, thank you."

Malcolm was going to return the question, but he could see they would not be wasting time on chit-chat.

"Good," said Mr. Bolton, clearing his throat. "So the last time we met, it was decided that you'd be reassigned to the ICA desk to help boost your overall performance score, which last time," he adjusted his glasses and leaned in close to the pad of paper he was writing on, "could benefit from improvement." He leaned back and steepled his fingers. "How do you feel that this has enhanced your daily work life?"

If the soul could sigh, Malcolm's would be out of breath. The ICA desk, or "the Hole" as it was commonly known among the herd, was where Pinnacle Insurance employed temps biannually to retrieve and purge old files and documents. In reality, it was where the trash was kept. Employees who needed to "maximize efficiency" or "focus on their career goals" were placed there. On either side of the Hole were two other cubicles packed nearly to the ceiling with boxes upon boxes of files, outdated computers and other defunct technology. And, sandwiched between them, was Employee #75376: Malcolm Moore.

These little sessions pained him, but unfortunately, they were necessary if he wanted to keep his job.

If only…

"So, Mister Moore, how would you describe your role in the workplace?"

"Well, basically I manage to thinly veil contempt for my superiors—that would be you—and all the other mindless drones by placing my real focus on daydreams of all the places I'd like to see before I die but can't afford on my salary."

"Splendid. And I take it your new assignment has given you ample time to devote to this pursuit?"

"Absolutely. It's all I can do in that broom closet with all the other junk. It has given me time to reflect on a few career goals, though."

"Such as?"

"Yours."

"Is that so?"

"Yes indeed."

"Would you care to enlighten me?"

"I'd be delighted! You see, this company hinges on the ability of its management to justify their 'integral position' by ensuring that at least fifteen percent of employees receive a negative review even though requirements are being met. Rather than use any kind of professional business model, this is achieved by cowing us into striving for lofty goals and then comparing us to each other.

"This has a two-pronged effect. One, it guarantees that some poor sap will wind up at the bottom—that would be me—and two, it obscures the fact that day after day we're being brainwashed by a group of people whose skills are really nothing more than the ability to mislead us by providing just enough information, but not so much that we'll catch on to your little charade."

"Hmmm, interesting. Not that it matters one way or the other, since your ass is mine. But I'm glad to see we understand each other."

"Speaking of which, shall I bend over now?"

"Yes, I think so."

They would both drop their pants, Mr. Bolton would position himself behind Malcolm, and begin to thrust.

"Next question: what is your job again?"

Malcolm gave Mr. Bolton every programmed answer he knew he wanted to hear. Eventually they became nothing more than a series of algorithms. Somewhere in there a glitch surfaced yet again from the endless code of ones and zeroes.

The shores of Spain.

The ebb and flow of the waves like the earth itself inhaling and exhaling. The sun on his face, the smell of the open sea, food so exquisite it could only have come from another world. He could buy a boat and live by the ocean, free of stress, bills, traffic, the worldly things powerless against his zest for life. As this memory died again with Mr. Bolton rambling on about third quarter mission statements, he wanted to die.

There was a knock at the door. A lazy, unusual knock.

"Yes?" said Mr. Bolton patiently.

No answer but three more languid thumps in a row. He cleared his throat again and rose to answer the door.

A hand shot through the opening as soon as there was enough space. It began to swipe and claw at whatever was near before a forceful blow hit the door, striking Mr. Bolton in the chest. His poor excuse for a toupee peeled back and hung like the party end of a mullet at the back of his head. He went stumbling backward until he connected hard with the desk and dropped to the floor.

Malcolm jumped out of his seat to see Zack darkening the doorway. No longer the smirking twerp, he was now primal and savage. His summer tan replaced with a clammy grey pallor the color of shark skin. He lumbered like a caveman in a hunched, almost simian manner, closer and closer to Mr. Bolton. His mouth had gone slack, drooling with each clumsy step, eyes demented and bloodshot.

"Hey!" Malcolm yelled. "Have you lost your mind?"

If Zack heard him, he gave no sign as he stretched one twisted hand and grabbed a winded and wheezing Mr. Bolton by his collar, wrenched his torso forward and bit him on the neck. Head jerking back and forth, he tore skin from bone and came up with a mouthful of jugular flesh.

"Oh my god." Malcolm was too shocked to even scream.

With little hair to grab, Zack had both fists grasped on both ears, moments away from cracking his skull into the corner of the desk like a piñata and feasting on the juicy candy inside.

The lamp came down with a sick, wet crunch and Zack collapsed on top of Mr. Bolton.

Malcolm towered over them, the lamp from his boss's desk clutched firmly in his hand. It was the first time he had killed someone. That didn't scare him. What scared him was how close he had come to letting the creep finish the job.

He tossed the lamp aside and rolled Zack's corpse off Mr.

Bolton. "Stan?" he yelled frantically. No answer. Blood spilled from the open hole in his neck and onto the cheap office carpet.

"Someone call the—" Malcolm called out in panic.

There was a growing din from the floor behind him. The place had descended into anarchy. Gnarled faces. Screams. People running this way and that. Each shirt marred by a loose tie or splatters of blood on their clothes that made them into hellish caricatures of themselves. The dinner bell had been rung. They were starving... and coming his way.

Malcolm slammed and locked the door as quickly as he could, moments before the pummeling of fists started on the other side. The only door, the only way out, was blocked by the living dead.

Malcolm began frantically looking around. The windows didn't open and there was nowhere worth hiding. He tried the phone, but it was dead as he would soon be. Eventually one of them would decide to throw a chair through the glass wall that had STAN BOLTON, REGIONAL MANAGER etched into it. Even if they didn't, he was still stuck in a room with his injured, bleeding, most likely infected boss. Malcolm was no horror buff, but he knew what usually came next. It's only a matter of time, he thought, before it works its way through the body and finally resurrects each corpse to feast on those around them.

Mr. Bolton wasn't quite done yet, still breathing a little. For all Malcolm knew, he could be breathing the virus out into the air right now.

The air!

Sure enough, a dusty air vent with chipped paint was positioned just above the oversized desk. As far as Malcolm was concerned, it was the pearly gates. He hoisted himself onto the big oak desk and reached for the vent, just able to reach it to find that the covering lifted from its resting place easily. The duct itself, however, was a tighter fit than he had hoped.

A hard crack came from the covered window. Then with one

good boost, he slipped inside just before the glass shattered and a chorus of moans filled the office below.

Crawling through an air duct wasn't the way it looked on TV. It was filthy, full of cobwebs and tight as a straitjacket.

A small square of light appeared ahead. Another vent.

He reached it and recoiled at the sight of a group of his former peers crowded around an office table, devouring poor Betty the way they would a cake when it was someone's birthday.

She was still alive. Twitching.

Computer screens throughout the floor flashed on and off, a single word blinking among the chaos in big red lettering.

BRAINS!...BRAINS!...BRAINS!

The longer he looked, the more he felt fixed by it, mesmerized the way a frog would be by the blinding glare of a flashlight. A tone began to sound just behind his eardrums, louder and louder, and the only thought in his head was of tasty grey matter.

Echoes of moaning sounded through the vent like the halls of a haunted house. Suddenly one stuck his head into the opening through which Malcolm had entered the duct and smiled a broken, blood-soaked grin.

Free of the spell, he crawled as fast as he could until safely out of reach. The ghoul clawed and scratched at the sides of the duct in rage, screeching on the metal, but couldn't muster the motor functions to crawl inside.

Malcolm took a deep breath of relief just as the vent below him whined and gave way, sending him hurling into the space below.

He fell hard on his left shoulder. A hard lump of air forced its way out of his lungs. Unopened mail littered the table he landed on. A handful of envelopes gently fluttered from the air. Dazed, the white ceiling above spun like a cyclone, the hole he fell through the eye in the centre of the storm.

There had been bad days in the past, but this easily took the gold medal.

Just as he was about to black out, a flat, grey object suddenly came flying toward his face. He yelled and heard what he thought was his echo, but was in fact that of another voice.

Malcolm sat up to see a frightened young man with long greasy hair who stunk of cigarettes brandishing a computer keyboard.

"Oh Malcolm, it's you," he said. "God! You scared the holy shit out of me, man."

"I was about to say the same." Malcolm rubbed his shoulder that now howled in agony, hopped off the table and faced the shaken mail guy. For all he knew they may have been the only two people who weren't turned into brain-starved office workers, but for the life of him Malcolm couldn't remember his name.

"What the hell's going on around here? I was about to do my rounds and walked into Dawn of the Dead. Barely got back here in one piece."

"I have no idea," said Malcolm, dizzily studying the cramped little mailroom. "One minute I was going through my monthly enema with my boss and next thing I know some nutcase burst in and bit him."

"Are you kidding?"

"I wish I were, but I—" Malcolm paused, remembering. "Wait! Before I left there was an e-mail. Zombie something-or-other." He looked around frantically. He had never been in here before, yet it felt familiar. The way it was packed with shelves of stationary and dusty boxes of Pinnacle Insurance envelopes and letterhead reminded him of his own. "Where's your computer?"

The mail guy pointed to a corner of the room. Sure enough the vague outline of a computer monitor was visible between stacks of boxes. Malcolm sat down, ready to type, but there was no keyboard until the mail guy plugged it back in and set it down in front of him.

"Thanks."

The screen sparked to life.

BRAINS!…BRAINS!…BRAINS!

The flashing, blood-red letters were followed by the high-pitched tone of a fax machine dialing a wrong number. Not in his ears, in his mind. Again came hungry thoughts, visions of soft flesh and snapping bones. Brain pudding… brain stew… brain tartare.

Suddenly the mail guy picked up the monitor and flung it as hard as he could, shattering it with a loud pop as a shower of plastic and glass fell on the floor.

"What the… what happened?" said Malcolm, shaking off the demented visions, the tone still echoing in his skull.

"What happened?" asked the mail guy, clearly unsettled. "You zoned out and started to moan like one of them."

"How can that be? It's just a computer."

"So are our brains, man. They don't take much to scramble. Is it so hard to believe that they can be reprogrammed too?"

Hard-to-believe was being redefined minute to minute.

"If so then why haven't we been infected with this… this virus?"

"A few more seconds and you probably would've been. It must be from exposure. Did you actually open the e-mail yourself?"

"No, I deleted it."

"Good idea."

"But somebody must have. Someone must have wanted to see what it was."

"Bad idea."

"Clearly," said Malcolm dryly. "The signal must spread through any hardware connected to it. Computers, phones, fax machines…"

"Us."

"Jesus!" said Malcolm in shock. "It could infect our other offices around the country."

"It probably already has."

"Great! So now what do we do?"

WHUMP!

Something hit the door. Then came the moans.

Cold goosebumps prickled up on the soft bottoms of Malcolm's arms. "They can't get in here, can they?"

The mail guy shook his head. "No way. The door's electronically locked." He began to trail off, not so sure now. They both gave each other the same look.

They scrambled for things to barricade the door with. Malcolm threw some nearby boxes behind the door just as the pounding of fists grew louder from the other side. A gap appeared between the door and its frame, the hungered moans sounding clearer with each bit of space.

The mail guy disappeared to the back and returned moments later with an aluminum ladder. "Here," he barked and slid the two pieces apart until it wedged horizontally into place between the door and opposing wall. "That should hold it... I think." Fists came hammering from the other side, louder than before.

The two of them backed away from the door with no choice but to listen to the growing commotion outside. It wasn't long before the sharp crack of splitting wood came from the frame.

"Can we get up there?" said the mail guy, pointing to the open vent in the ceiling.

"Not without the ladder," said Malcolm. "Besides, I don't think we want to go that way."

Another crack louder than the first.

"Well, we don't want to be here either!" It sounded like they were tearing their way in, gnawing at the drywall like a swarm of rats. "What do we do?"

"What can we do?" Malcolm sighed with defeat.

Silence fell across them both. Big questions, little time.

The mail guy collapsed into a nearby chair. He took a pack of cigarettes from his shirt pocket, took one out and lit it. Malcolm leaned against the wall, the shock now blooming into real fear.

He knew perfectly well that he would rather take his own life than become one of them.

Spain, he thought sadly to himself. *I should be in Spain.*

He looked around. What could he use? He could lick his fingers and stick them in the wall socket. There was the window of course, but he'd have to break the glass with something. The computer? No, he would need the chair. There was a whole box of extension cords on one of the shelves nearby; he could make a noose and...

He took a step back and looked at the rows of metal shelves and everything on them. Office supplies, mostly—scissors, letter openers, paper cutters, pens, pencils and liquid paper. On another row were all sorts of maintenance equipment like duct tape, hammers, nails, screwdrivers, a few cans of WD-40, a nail gun and a fire extinguisher.

"We can fight."

"What?" said the mail guy, coughing smoke.

Malcolm turned and faced him. "We can fight!" he repeated, and began gathering up everything in sight. "I don't know about you, but I am not dying in this hell hole. I say we grab everything that will kill and give 'em hell!"

The idea sunk in, and with the sound of snapping wood he too sprang into action.

Armfuls of supplies were hauled from the shelves until they covered the floor. Malcolm kept the nail gun for himself, pried the two blades of a pair of scissors apart and held one in each fist. Not much, but if thrust hard enough they'd make short work of his attacker's eyes. He stood and saw that his comrade had fashioned a spear out of a broom and several pairs of scissors duct taped to one end. He had also made a makeshift flail out of power cords and a triangular Pinnacle paper weight tucked into his belt.

Another crack and Malcolm's chest tightened against his pounding heart, knowing the moment was close and it had not long left to beat.

With his spear tucked under one arm, the mail guy moved ahead holding the bright red fire extinguisher, aiming the nozzle toward the door, bent now from its frame and crushing the ladder under its weight.

"When they come in I'm going to blast them with this. Then you let 'em have it. Okay?"

"Okay," said Malcolm, clenching the nail gun. For better or worse, he was ready. "One last thing…what's your name?"

"Darrell."

"Sorry."

He shrugged. "Happens all the time."

The door gave way. They poured in, trampling over the fallen door as if it were never there. Mangled faces appeared and went from lazy stares to desperate grins at the sight of fresh meat. Darrell fired the extinguisher when they were close, hitting each one of them with a damp, white fog.

Malcolm shot. He missed. He shot again. He missed again. Several more, but he only hit one.

"DIE!" he shouted, dropping the nail gun and pulling the scissor blades from his pockets. With the first thrust of metal into bloated, grey skin, Malcolm became a berserker. They dropped like flies at the business end of his fury. Dark brown blood oozed from the wounds and gashes as he poured all his hate and rage, every memory, every ounce of lost time into his blows. He would not have recognized the person weaving between them cutting each one down with the ease of a trained samurai.

When it was over he stood triumphant over at least a dozen corpses. Panting. Sweaty. Freckled with clotted blood. A new man.

"Way to go, Ash!" said Darrell as he clapped Malcolm on the back. He'd been mending his bent bloody spear with duct tape. A small totem of lifeless corpses lay at his feet.

"Huh?"

"Never mind." He stepped carefully over the bodies. "Let's make like a tree and get the fuck out of here!"

"I don't know," said Malcolm as he gingerly peaked around the corner of the door frame. "How do we know it's safe?"

A face, one he never wished to see again, came hurling at him, buried itself in his shoulder and bit. The late Mr. Bolton, reanimated and ferocious, gnawed and gnashed, trying to separate flesh from bone. It was surreal, being eaten. Especially by your boss whose hairpiece still clung on for dear life, swaying back and forth as he chewed.

Blood rushed in Malcolm's ears so loud he barely heard Darrell yell as he thrust the nail gun over his shoulder and planted one in Mr. Bolton's forehead point blank. He dropped like a bundle of wet rope.

Malcolm fell hard against the wall, pain shooting through him already despite the adrenaline.

"Son of a bitch!" said Darrell with disgust.

"Is it bad?" said Malcolm breathlessly, straining his neck to get a better look. From the shoulder and all down the sleeve was wet with blood. A ragged flap of torn material hung loose where he'd been bit. Through the hole, two nasty, crescent-shaped teeth marks were visible.

Malcolm winced with pain as he squirmed out of his ruined shirt. Darrell helped by tying it as tight as he could over the wound to stop the bleeding.

"Thanks," said Malcolm. "But I think it's too late."

"Don't say that. It may not be like the movies. We don't know for sure that you'll turn into one of them."

"Yes we do," he interrupted, nodding toward his attacker. "That was my boss."

"Shit." The grave reality of the situation hit all the way home now. "Shall I… you know… do the honors?" Darrell gestured to the nail gun on the floor next to them.

Malcolm thought about it for a moment. "I don't want to die here. Just help me get out of here first. That's all I ask."

"You got it." He put the nail gun in Malcolm's good hand. "Here. You'll probably need it more than me."

Darrell helped Malcolm up off the floor. He hissed through his teeth as he rose, but finally made it to his feet.

"Maybe I should go first," Malcolm suggested. "In case there are more of them."

"Be my guest."

He entered the hallway to see it was deserted, but behind every door, around every corner he expected to see mangled, ravenous faces. The very thought made Malcolm's stomach clench up with disgust. Or was that hunger?

Darrell followed carefully, slowly as they made their way to the elevator. Malcolm pressed the down button with the butt of the nail gun. It didn't light up. He tried a few more times.

"Looks like we're taking the stairs."

"I'm not so sure that's a good idea."

"Why?"

"Think about it. There are three hundred people in this building, we've seen maybe twenty between the two of us."

Malcolm shrugged impatiently.

"So where's everyone else?"

"I don't know," said Malcolm. "And I'm not wasting my last few minutes waiting to find out!" With that he sped back down the hall and toward the stairwell door. Darrell shouted for him to wait, but it did no good. Malcolm burst into the stairwell, his footsteps clapping loudly off its concrete walls, the building itself spinning out of control at a dizzying pace as he hurried down the steps.

Five…

Four…

Three…

Two…

Finally he reached the ground level and stopped at a door marked by a large letter G. On the other side of the door he heard what sounded like fireworks exploding. Malcolm took a deep breath, braced himself and flung open the door.

Hell, it seemed, had found its way to the main reception area of Pinnacle Insurance. An entire army of haggard dead filled the main reception area, not a living soul among them. One was missing his legs, cut down at the kneecaps, and he crawled ahead with his hands, his black tongue reaching out for a taste of the nearest succulent flesh. The plate glass that had spanned the whole north wall was now broken and littered across the floor. Police surrounded the front entrance outside, shielding themselves behind cruisers, shouting into handheld radios, firing shot after shot at the oncoming horde. A pair of them reached a young rookie who had foolishly got too close and were pulling on both arms as though he were a wishbone at Thanksgiving dinner.

The hail of gunfire thinned the herd, but still they advanced, still they lurched forward.

And Malcolm was becoming one of them. He could feel it, the growing, ceaseless hunger as his body succumbed to the infection. His heartbeat slowed to a peculiar spasm in his chest. His vision began to shift values, light to dark like the negative of a photograph as he became a drone, a spare part, a copy of a copy of a copy. He could hear them now, their single collective thought that surged in his mind.

Brains.

Brains!

BRAINS!!!

With his last few scraps of humanity, Malcolm Moore tightened his grip on the nail gun, let out a mighty war cry and charged into the horrible crush of bodies. His final thoughts were of blue water, white shores and a golden yellow sunset.

A memory reduced to nothing more than an old postcard he'd kept for far too long.

ACTS OF VIOLENCE

Ever had that one job that just sucks the soul, the sanity, and the will to live right out of you? That's about the size of it here. We spend so much of our lives—time we'll never get back—at our jobs. In pointless meetings. Listening to one co-worker or another drone on about banalities like the weather or weekend plans and somewhere in the process, lose ourselves. We were meant for something more than this.

At least, I think so.

JUST ONE OF THOSE THINGS

The house was on a street called Grove Cove, a tree-lined cul-de-sac of a merry little suburban neighborhood. The tall, ripe maples cast a pleasantly cool shade but not so much as to block out the late morning sun. A two-storey, modern concept house, complete with a two-car garage and flower bed lining the path from the driveway to the front door. Very much the same as the neighboring houses: same shape, same size, same colors. The only thing that made it any different was the red and white FOR SALE sign planted in the fresh green grass of the front lawn.

A car pulled up and slowed to a crawl as its occupants scanned the exterior from within.

"It's the right house," said Lacey as she leaned closer to the windshield, straining to see the numbers 712 above the garage door. "Doesn't look like anyone's here though."

"Well, we are a bit early," Jon replied after checking his watch, a hint of conceit in his voice. He pulled the car into the driveway and silenced it with a twist of the keys.

They both got out past the spot where the sign stood like a cross in a grave on this deserted but otherwise picturesque street.

She short and pretty, but not in an obvious, beauty pageant way, he well-built and passably handsome, not the type you'd cross the street for but enough to say so. Both of them dressed casually, but stylishly.

"This is nice," Lacey said, adjusting her glasses as she took a leisurely scan of the neighborhood. A few houses down, a sprinkler, the old fan type she remembered from her childhood, sprayed its elegant wave of water across the lawn and part of the sidewalk. She could almost see children leaping through it, drawing animals on the pavement with chalk, eating ice cream. Kids being kids.

"Uh-huh," grunted Jon as he leaned coolly against the car, thumbing through old text messages. Everything about him said he didn't want to be here. Lacey narrowed her gaze at him and moved closer, waiting. He stuck his phone back in the front pocket of his faded jeans.

"Yes, it's nice," he said with more conviction this time, panning across the house's siblings on either side. *So were the other six we've seen so far.* The thought came dangerously close to escaping his lips. They had begun to blur together, the other houses. There were two in Etobicoke, two in Mississauga, and one each in Brampton and Oakville. Each one quaint and cozy; the perfect place for nice, decent people who wanted to hang their hats and start a family, and none of them compared to the townhouse they were leaving downtown.

What's left of it, anyway.

"Picture it," Lacey said as she sidled up against him with a big dewy grin, bumping her hip into his. "Just the two of us here… and eventually," she pressed her body up against his, "maybe a third."

"Sounds good," Jon smiled back, slipping his right hand into her back pocket as he kissed her waiting lips. Their minds were in the same place for the first time since they began house hunting, though for Jon the appeal was more the making of a baby and not so much the having of one. He checked his watch again. "Okay, let's see what the deal is here."

They left the driveway and started toward the front door.

"Maybe we should give him a call," said Lacey, rooting through her purse as she climbed the front steps of the porch. "What's the name, again?"

Jon, just behind her, looked at the sign on the front lawn. "Ed Slydell. Four, one, six…"

Cell phone in hand, she began dialing the number as it was read aloud to her. When she faced the door again, Lacey jumped backward and let out a yelp.

Someone was standing in the front window.

The front door unlocked with a metallic click and opened to reveal a man dressed in a simple grey suit and tie. His face was full if a bit pale, cheeks hugging his rounded chin. Clean-shaven, hair styled back smoothly, with a practiced smile putting his second-to-none pearly whites on full display.

"Well, hello there!" His mouth moved just long enough to utter the words before reverting to the impenetrable shield of white teeth.

"You must be Ed," said Jon.

"I guess I must be," he said with a chuckle. The man stuck out his hand.

"I'm Jon." He shook Ed's hand. "This is my fiancée, Lacey."

Ed offered his hand to her as well. "A pleasure to meet you both! Thanks for coming."

"Are we too early?" said Jon.

Ed waved the question away. "Not at all! Please come in."

"Oh wow," said Lacey upon entering the foyer.

The floor was immaculate ash grey tile. There were four rooms off the main hallway—a living room, dining room, kitchen and what appeared to be a den. A staircase ahead hugged the wall and wound its way up to the second floor with a well-made railing leading the way. There was a door in the foyer, just off the main hall, presumably to the basement. The whole place smelled of paint, fresh as the risen sun. All of it pure white as virgin snow.

"Beautiful property, isn't it?" said Ed with the widest smile you ever did see. "Let me show you around."

"Yeah, it's a nice space," Jon offered very generally.

They made their way casually through the main floor. The living room consisted of an iron-framed fireplace made of red brick, adjoining the den with a pair of French doors. A good amount of natural light was let in from the two large windows, warming the hardwood. The kitchen was complete with marble countertops, a stainless steel hood over the oven, and a refrigerator that looked to be brand new. All of it without so much as a scrap of furniture.

Empty houses echo in a way ones being lived in don't. But rather than talk, all the walls did at the moment was reflect their own voices back to them. Naked and silent, they told no story.

Not yet, at least.

Lacey filled the empty spaces with one item or another, mentally cutting things from the pages of a catalog and sticking them where she saw fit. Many things, most, in fact, were lost in the fire and they had held off replacing them until there was somewhere to put them. There, between the two windows, would be a good place to put a sideboard. And in front of the fireplace, a new sofa. They could always get a new dining room set, and a new coffee table, maybe even that decorative bird cage she saw at Pier One. Yes, this would do nicely.

"Brand new?" she asked.

"Ah, no, a few years old actually but recently refurbished." Ed smoothed the front of his suit. "But you can't beat the value."

"Yeah, we were wondering about that," said Jon. "Why so cheap? A house like this could easily go for twice, maybe even three times as much."

"Well, just between us," Ed leaned in close and placed his

palm at one side of his mouth for effect, "the owner is highly motivated."

"Any idea why?" Lacey asked.

"A move to the Maritimes, I believe."

"Oh, Jon's from there originally."

"Really?" said Ed, sounding genuinely interested. Or at least, if he wasn't he did a fine job of making it seem so. "Whereabouts?"

"Halifax," Jon answered.

"Marvellous. Beautiful area, isn't it?"

"Sure is." Jon gestured at the rest of the house. "Mind if we just have a look around?"

"Of course! Just let me know if you need anything at all." With that Ed took out his phone and stood sentry in the foyer as he began to tap at it.

"This guy's something, huh?" Jon said just under his breath.

Lacey noticed Ed watching them from the kitchen, just across the hallway. That plastic howdy neighbor grin still spread across his face.

"He gives me the creeps a little bit," she said.

"He's a realtor. They're all a little weird." He took his phone from his pocket again to check the time.

Lacey pondered a moment. "Are they?"

"Yeah. Sure." Quickly lost in some app.

She gave him a look all husbands have seen from their wives —*the* look—and folded her arms. Unamused.

"What?"

"It would be nice if you were a little more present while choosing our future home."

"Baby, what do you want me to say? I like it. I liked the last one. And the one before."

The look intensified.

Jon put away his phone. "I'll try to be a little more enthusiastic."

"Thank you. In the meantime, I think I'll have a look around on my own."

"Fine."

They each went their separate ways; him toward the backyard, her toward the staircase.

Thank Christ, Jon thought. *Give me two seconds of peace away from her cloying attention.* He loved her, or he had at one point, but now…it was just too much.

He was tired of her insistence. Her domestic overbearance. Her frequent hounding him to have kids. Sometimes it was all more than he could bear. And now with their townhouse burning down, something had changed in him. He'd called in a few favors to have it kept discreet, but the fire wasn't from a bad fuse like it said on the report. It was from her leaving her goddamn curling iron on. He had told her about that. So many times. If anyone found out they wouldn't have been able to collect the insurance money. And now with her pushing to move out of downtown. He liked the downtown. But that wasn't the only reason. It's where Kayla was.

He had met her at O'Sullivan's, a bar that a lot of guys from the station frequented on Dundas. If the tight jeans, low-cut top, and curly black hair wasn't enough, one look of those fuck-me eyes and the fact that he was a fireman sure was. He said maybe they should take things back to her place…and she said, "Why wait?" with a flick of her eyebrows to the bathroom.

The rest was history.

She gave him everything Lacey didn't. Excitement, freedom, no expectations. She didn't even make him wear a condom most of the time. With Lacey, the sex was fine but "safe" and ever since her wanting kids he found himself wanting her less. Kayla was willing to do it on the roof of a hotel. An elevator. A movie theatre. He soon became a junkie for it.

And now that could soon be over if they moved. And here she was asking him to be more enthusiastic.

Enthusiastic? After his home of ten years burned down because of her. He had been in burning buildings and never felt the same pressure and suffocation he got from her.

Did the city have its flaws? Sure. It was mostly safe unless you took a real wrong turn at the wrong time of night. Though occasionally he would get the feeling that someone was following him and then realize that it was nothing. Just a stranger walking too close or going the same direction. Awkward but harmless.

And he'd give in too. Ultimately, he knew it. All she would have to do was give him that look, call him "honey" in that sweet drawn-out way of hers, and that would be that.

Still, the place was nice enough. Might be worth it just to get things over with.

Maybe...

Through the living room window at the front of the house, Jon saw a car pull into the driveway next door. Out came an absolutely stunning woman with a purse slung over one arm. Her silky brown hair bounced as she stepped and the sunglasses she wore somehow made her look all the more incredible as she disappeared inside.

Might definitely *be worth it.*

"Honestly," said Lacey under her breath as soon as Jon was far enough away. She began climbing the stairs to the second floor. Five doors lined the hallway, all of them open. A master bedroom, two smaller ones, a bathroom, and a spare room that could be used for an office or playroom or guest room, anything really.

Could he be any more disinterested? And that wasn't all he was losing interest in. She could tell. No matter how much she loved him, no matter how she took an interest in him and his interests at the sacrifice of her own, no matter how she kept herself fit, tried to make a nice home, did her best to please him, it was never enough.

It wasn't long before she got suspicious, and then hired a private investigator to follow him when he said he was "working late." Well, he was working alright...working some slut in Liberty Village. When Lacey got the envelope she didn't even open it at first. She couldn't. She was afraid to. At just the thought of it her heart began to race. Then one evening while he was out, she couldn't take it anymore. Seeing the photos of them together—doing it in public places—it broke her. She wound up sitting on the edge of the bathtub staring into space while the world spiraled around her. The next thing she knew the smoke alarm was going off.

Lacey hurried to get the fire extinguisher...and somewhere along the way...stopped. *Let there be a fire. Let the place burn.*

If that's what it took to get his attention. She told him that she panicked, got scared as soon as there was smoke and did just what she was supposed to do when there's a fire: get out and call the fire department. And that's what she did. Just left out a few details like exactly when she noticed the fire, and how she could clearly see flames in the windows before making the call, and how it actually pleased her to see fire. Just a matter of details. No big deal, right? Okay, so the townhouses on either side had gotten a little singed and the families that lived in them had to leave, but no one was hurt. Scared to death maybe but not the end of the world. The city was a cesspool, she had always thought so. Wouldn't have lived there if it weren't for Jon already having a place. The further away from it, the better.

And this house seemed perfect. The others they had seen were fine, but this one had the right feel. The right vibe. It was close to the right schools and shopping centers and the right distance away from Liberty Village. Oh yes, this was the one. She would see to it. She knew just what to say and how to say it.

Lacey entered one of the smaller rooms, next to the master

bedroom, and looked out the window. *This could be the baby's room.* She so wanted a baby. Not a kid, definitely not a teenager, but a baby for sure. One day, it would be her turn. She would be the one to take pictures of them in cute little outfits, post them, have people tell her how cute he or she was, and how cute they were together, and what a cute family she had. The perfect family. The perfect life.

Who that baby was with, well…

In a perfect world she would keep looking for someone more suitable. But she had spent three years in this relationship, invested in it, and wasn't about to just give it all up now. Thirty was not so far away, and if she wanted this to happen, she couldn't afford to waste time. And if Jon continued to lose interest…a fake pregnancy ought to do it. Followed by a fake miscarriage. But a real one was in order one day soon. She had already stopped taking birth control, unbeknownst to Jon. Nor did he know that she had been poking holes in his condoms for months now, but that was before she found out about his side piece. No way in hell was *she* going to have his baby!

Hopefully this place she wouldn't have to burn down too. Even just the thought of it—the heat, the smell of smoke, the image in her mind of seeing all these white painted walls blackened and curled from flames—excited her a little.

No, must not do that. Not again.

A creak came from the floor behind her.

Lacey turned to see Ed standing there in the doorway behind her. Smiling. An unwelcome prickle went through her, and without realizing it, she held her breath.

"Finding your way around okay?" said Ed.

"Uh…yeah." A slight quiver in her voice. "Thanks."

Smiles come in all shapes and sizes. On the faces of friends, family, colleagues, lovers, even babies. Universal signs of joy. Contentment. That's not what Ed's smile said. Not at all.

Ed stepped inside the room. Without meaning to, Lacey took a step back.

"Beautiful property, isn't it?" Ed said, breaking the awkward silence.

"Yeah, I was just thinking that." Lacey began to fidget.

The corners were too wide, lasted too long, showed too many teeth to be normal. His smile said something was wrong. And his eyes were not smiling at all. His eyes were begging. The more she looked at it, the deeper the disquiet in her became.

"There's nothing wrong with it, is there?" She tried to make it sound like she was half kidding.

"Oh heavens, no!" He bursted out in an awkward fit of phony laughter. "Nothing's wrong. Not at all."

Ed took a step toward the window. Toward her. It was only now that she fully realized just how pale he was.

"Everything's fine." He was saying it more to himself than to her.

And it was true. Some houses are drafty, or stuffy, or have a smell you just can't quite put your finger on. But not this one. This one was just right.

Ed on the other hand, she wasn't so sure.

Jon appeared at the top of the stairs behind him.

Lacey went to him as he approached. Something about the way Ed was positioned in the room made her feel, for a moment, like he wasn't going to let her pass. Thankfully, she was wrong. He also didn't move as he stood directly in front of the door, leaving ample room behind for one to pass. She edged around him, and as she did saw a tiny bead of sweat form at his temple.

"There you are," said Lacey, trying not to make her relief too obvious. She looped her arm through his.

"Finding your way around okay?" Ed repeated.

"Yeah, it's a great place." He couldn't deny that it was pretty perfect. *Emphasis on pretty.*

"Well, what do you think, *honey?*"

There it was. Whether it was that or the collective pressure from the pair of plasticine smiles he was faced with, he couldn't say. Whatever the cause, the next words out of his mouth were, "I think we'll take it."

Now it was Jon's turn to fake a smile.

"Terrific!" said Ed.

"We'll talk things over and have an offer soon."

"An offer," said Ed, suppressing a slight fidget. "Right. Yes, of course. Sounds like a plan." He looked at his watch. "Uh, I do have another appointment though. The house will still technically be on the market after all. Hope you don't mind."

"Not at all," said Jon.

Ed began to lead back toward the front door when Lacey stopped in the foyer.

"Oh, what about the basement?"

Ed froze just as his hand fell on the doorknob. "Right," he said after a brief pause, though not brief enough. "Of course. Let's have a look at the basement."

He led the way through the foyer and to the door off the main hall and down they went. At the bottom Ed flicked on the light, bringing a series of uncovered bulbs to life. Jon and Lacey walked around as Ed went and stood in front of the only door down there.

Unfurnished like the rest of the place, and mostly unfinished. The walls, however, rather than left lined only with pink fiberglass insulation, had been drywalled. Plenty of storage in the crawl space under the stairs.

"As you can see it's the perfect area for an entertainment area or games room. A *man cave*, if you like." Ed gave Jon a light nudge with his elbow.

"What about this room?"

"Which room?"

"The one you're standing in front of," said Jon, gesturing behind him.

"Oh, I believe it's being used for storage."

"Can we see it anyway?"

A moment of visible hesitation, well concealed but not quite well enough, and Ed stepped aside. The door was fitted with a latch and padlock.

Jon reached for it. Ed didn't try to stop him.

It was unlocked and unhooked from the latch easily.

"Oh no."

Jon twisted the doorknob.

"No no!" Ed protested, clearly not aware of this fact. But it was too late. Jon opened the door.

The room was full of people. Not the common way one might find such a thing, spread out, standing casually on both legs. Instead, a nebulous mass of twisted faces, torsos and limbs, writhing against one another like a nest of snakes filled the space from floor to ceiling. All naked. All bloody. All screaming in silent agony. Near enough for Jon to reach out and put a finger through the empty void that was their eyes if he wished. Spots of blood spurted against his face, vanishing as fast as they appeared. Between them a network of thorned black veins wove between and pierced through them, serving as the thread that knit this grotesque tapestry. All of it undulating and slick with blood that seemed to drip downward, upward, sideward, and every other direction. A wave of cold like the inside of a meat locker swept out, as did the most concentrated stench of death. The pained utterance of each mouth within repeated the same word...

"Yum yum...Yum yum...Yum yum...Yum yum...Yum yum...Yum yum...Yum yum...Yum yum..."

Lacey, standing nearby, froze in stunned horror. A scream began to surface in her chest but was choked back before it could reach her throat.

Jon, disgusted and bewildered by the scene before him, finally slammed the door shut once his senses returned to him. He and Lacey turned and looked slowly at Ed.

His smile had gone from phony to nervous. Without a word, he took off running up the stairs.

Lacey chased after him, taking the steps two at a time, with Jon close behind. Feet pounded up the wooden steps in a race for the top.

Ed made it up first, naturally, through the door and slammed it shut just in time to see Lacey's face, terrified that she had come in second place, disappear behind it. He put his full weight flat against it.

"Okay, so full disclosure," Ed's voice said through the door, "the house has a little bit of a history."

"No fucking shit!" Jon shouted.

"I know it's unorthodox, but truthfully so long as you just don't go in that room, you hardly even notice."

"Are you crazy?" Lacey shrieked in disbelief.

"Tell you what? I'll even knock another twenty percent off the asking price."

"You'll knock?" she said before the penny dropped. "What do you mean... *you're* the owner?"

"Seriously, it's not that big a deal. It's just one of those things. One teeny tiny little quirk. Like Pop Pop's tool shed that no one was ever, *ever* allowed into. Just don't talk about it, don't disturb it, and it will all be okay."

"Says the guy trying to break free of it! Let us the fuck out *right now!*" Jon bellowed.

Behind them the prickle of cold could be felt, as could the horrible smell from a moment ago.

"You don't understand! I can't have any kind of a life."

A low ugly mutter had begun behind them. The crowd, little more than the shapes of heads, staggered out the now wide-open door. The veined mass spread out around the doorframe, corroding it like rust around a drain, and across the floor beneath them with each step they took. They were not altogether "there," these creatures. Figures shaped in the two-legged form of people but made of entirely different stuff. No flesh or bones. Drops of a viscous plasm fell against gravity from the mass below, forming a bloody exposed musculature, allowing them to lurch forward in a choppy, mucilaginous shamble. Intuitively molding itself upward into mouths capable of producing one sound.

"Yum yum...Yum yum...Yum yum..."

"I've had specialists, scientists, priests, Militia Dei. *Everyone!* No one can explain it. All I know is something bad is here and it can't leave."

"Yum yum...Yum yum...Yum yum..."

"I can't eat!"

"Yum yum...Yum yum...Yum yum..."

"I can't sleep!"

"Yum yum...Yum yum...Yum yum..."

"And I can't leave either!"

As a deep groan issued from the house itself, Jon and Lacey saw blood start to drip down from above, filling the carved paneling of the door before them. It leaked down from the frame like a breach in a bulkhead, but not at random. It took form, this blood, shaping itself into letters...

The haunted tongues uttering their ravenous plea filled the narrow stairway as they drew nearer. The impact of their approaching steps could be felt in the connected wood of the stairs beneath them. Crawling along the walls and ceiling above. Slowly, sporadically, like marionettes each led by a palsied hand.

Lacey looked at Jon. "Together?"

He looked back. "Together."

Then, as one, they pushed on one side of the door with all their combined strength, smearing the single arterial word, staining their clothes with it. On the other side of the door, Ed was unable to hold them any longer and toppled backward.

Two pairs of feet went racing past and didn't look back. He scrambled to his feet and chased after them. By the time he got to the driveway, the car peeled out, tires smoking and squealing as it did.

"Come back!" he shouted, each syllable more harrowed than the next. "Come back!" It was no use. They sped through the cul-de-sac and disappeared around the corner as far and as fast as they could.

Ed fell to his knees. Broken, defeated, dismayed, and exhausted from all those things.

Those things.

For more than a year now he had been living with *those things*. Those things which were dumped on to him by the last owner, and presumably the one before that. Who knew how far back it went? Maybe they were here before there was a house. Before there were people.

It was his fault really. He had found the house, he had pushed for it, he had opted to stay. Even when his wife threatened to leave—and then eventually did—he stayed. Now he felt like he was one of them.

Ed trudged back into the house and shuffled inside. Once the door was closed, he leaned his head upon it and wept. Tears of fatigue, frustration, and fear.

It was short lived.

"Yum yum?"

He turned and saw them. All huddled together in a horrid mass. One that was now spreading throughout the house, unconfined.

They wouldn't let him have a moment of peace. Not even one. All night and all day they hounded him with that same phrase of theirs.

"Yum yum...Yum yum...Yum yum..."

Ed had no clue what they wanted for the longest time. Had he not cut himself shaving one day he never would have. He had tried tempting them with raw meat from the butcher's, but without the right juice, they had no interest in it. And he dared not try raw *human* meat. That was just unthinkable.

Ed went to the fridge and took out a pint of blood. His blood. Given little by little. Sometimes even when locked up they made a sound, if they were hungry enough. He slowly dribbled it along the floor. The second it landed the blood was lapped up as if it had simply disappeared into the grouting between tiles. They dropped and greedily drank it up, leaving not so much as a speckle, and their hungered plea stopped.

Ed let more out and began down into the basement again. They followed.

Costly as far as bait goes, but we do what we have to. Back into the room he led them. The black veined mass and the cold that came with it. Ed dropped the remainder of the blood in the middle of the room and they swarmed it like sharks to chum.

Ed shut the door immediately behind him, and this time, locked it. Properly. Firmly. Certainly. He pulled on the padlock itself three times to make sure there was no mistaking it. He slid down against the door until he was sitting on the cold, hard concrete. Head in his hands and staring away into nothing.

So close. I was so close!

It didn't matter now. All he could do now was try again. And try he would, until he succeeded or went completely stark raving mad, which didn't feel so far away.

Maybe that wouldn't be the worst thing, he thought. He didn't care anymore. Let them escape. Let them tell others of what horror awaited them at number 712 Grove Cove. Maybe then someone would come and take him away to a nice padded room with some lovely drugs to mute the mutter of haunted tongues he heard no matter how far from the house he was. Then again, maybe not.

Ed crawled to his feet and stamped back up to the main floor. Courtesy of the front hall bathroom mirror, he straightened his loose tie, smoothed back his disheveled hair, and dabbed every bit of perspiration on his face and neck with a nearby hand towel. And the final touch—his usual glass-cutting smile.

There, that's better. He had to look his best, after all. His twelve o'clock appointment would be arriving soon.

Haunted houses are a trope that have been, if you'll pardon the pun, done to death. That doesn't mean they can't be done well, but either way, many tend to follow a similar type of formula — family moves into old house with a history, haunting becomes progressively more evident, ghosts want family out, family leaves. This story differs from that formula in one notable way: the house doesn't want people out, it wants them to stay. It needs them to stay. It won't let them go. Also I decided to show what happens before a family can actually move in. I remember this occurring to me while watching one particular haunted house movie (which I can't recall) and thought what if this takes a few tries? What if other people were scared off because whatever is haunting this particular dwelling rattled their chains while they were trying to picture themselves living there? That would send just about anyone running. However, from the way this story ended, it implies that maybe the next people to view the house won't be quite so lucky…

STAY WITH ME

"How bad is the bleeding?"

"Where is the smoke coming from?"

"Is he urinating on himself right now?"

"Sir, could you speak up please?"

"Ma'am, could you stop yelling?"

"Okay, help is on the way."

. . .

These stray words all mingled together with the rapid tapping of computer keys throughout the call center. There were always a few incidents this time of year: mostly noise complaints and vandals, a few fights, a car accident, the occasional report of clowns lurking in the dark trying to scare people. But so far, it was a pretty quiet night for Halloween.

The incoming call could have gone to anyone. Had it been made a millionth of a second earlier, it would have gone to Ron, currently speaking to a distraught mother whose son hadn't come home from trick-or-treating. A millisecond later and it would have gone to Janice, who had just finished a call and was logged out for a break. But instead, electricity shot through the wires connected to the phone of Nina Wallace.

Her monitor blinked to life.

OPERATOR: Nine-one-one, what's your emergency?
CALLER: Yes, um…

Male. Not a deep voice, not high either. Age and race were hard to determine over the phone, but not impossible. That was about all she could make out, other than that he sounded like he was trying not to be heard.

CALLER: I'd like to report a murder.

Oh god. This was it. The call Nina had feared she would receive one day. The one she'd had to make herself, once.

She took a deep breath to steady herself.

OPERATOR: Okay, just stay with me alright?
CALLER: Don't worry, I'm not going anywhere.
OPERATOR: Can you give me a location?
CALLER: Ten thirty-one Darrow Street.

Nina's fingers flew across the keyboard.

OPERATOR: Is that a house, or an apartment?
CALLER: A house.

He was calm. Way more than she might have expected. Shock could do that to people sometimes, she had seen it before. But why was he whispering?

OPERATOR: Can you see the assailant right now?
CALLER: Not at the moment, no.
OPERATOR: Are you somewhere safe?
CALLER: Oh yes, I'm safe. Perfectly safe.
OPERATOR: Good. One moment. Just stay on the line. You're doing really well.
CALLER: Thank you.

Nina sent for the nearest unit to respond immediately.

She never forgot the sight of her sister lying there face down on their living room floor, the back of her head bashed in. So cold. So...gone. Then a shadow swept across the floor followed by heavy footsteps. She saw a man with long dark hair, mechanic's coveralls, and a beard standing by the front door. He was holding a bloody hammer. They stared at each other for a moment while he wiped his feet on the doormat like any considerate guest would. Then he just left.

OPERATOR: Alright, the police are on their way. Is this a friend or family member?
CALLER: Neither.
OPERATOR: Then how do you know them?
CALLER: I don't. *inaudible* I was just passing by.
OPERATOR: Are you inside the house right now?
CALLER: No, I'm outside. At the moment.

OPERATOR: Can you see the victim?
CALLER: Oh yes. I can see her.
OPERATOR: Can you give me a description?
CALLER: Brunette. Late thirties, early forties. Size seven, I think. *inaudible* Lovely throat.

No response from either end. A moment which dropped the ugliest chill right in her gut.

OPERATOR: Sir, I need you to tell me exactly what happened.
CALLER: What happened?
OPERATOR: Yes.
CALLER: What happened is a man with a knife found an unlocked door. That's what happened.
OPERATOR: When did—
CALLER: Tonight, of all nights.
OPERATOR: Sir, when did this happen?

...

OPERATOR: Sir?

All she could hear from the other end was a few short clicks, muffled footsteps, and a scream cut short by gurgling sounds Nina wouldn't be able to forget as long as she lived. They went on for longer than she expected. And when they finally stopped...

CALLER: Just now.

He still sounded calm.

This was the second story I ever had accepted to a submission call and I wrote it the same day I submitted it. I don't remember exactly where it came from but at least part of the inspiration for it was a Richard Matheson story called Nearly Departed. *It was one of those horror stories where the whole way through there's really nothing obviously horrifying about it…until you get to the end.*

DOLL

IN HIS TWENTY-FIVE YEARS ON THE FORCE, DETECTIVE O'Shea had seen many disturbing things, but nothing could have prepared him for the strange case of Dennis Kowalski.

He arrived at Bellevue Hospital around six o' clock. He knew it well. Bellevue had hosted the birth of both his children, the death of his father from prostate cancer, and many an unfortunate victim from the cases he's investigated. Tonight, however, his business was in a part of the hospital he had never been to before.

The psychiatric ward.

He was a tall man, solidly built with a smooth chin where there used to be two-day stubble, with red hair that was fading to grey just above the ears. Doctors and nurses went about their business throughout the corridor. Past a row of green chairs, he finally reached the reception area. Behind the window, a young girl with glasses and braces was quietly doing a Sudoku puzzle. The tag on her scrubs said her name was Lisa.

O'Shea took his badge from his coat pocket, flipped it open and tapped the glass with it. "I'm here to see a patient."

"Name?" she asked, swinging her chair over to the computer.

"Kowalski," said O'Shea.

Away she tapped at her keyboard until the screen came up. "Dennis?"

"That's him."

"He's been transferred to the EOU."

O'Shea shrugged. "Meaning?"

"Extended Observation," said a voice to his left. A short, olive-skinned man with a cup of coffee in one hand and a file folder in the other came to a halt next to him. "Good to see you, Rick."

"Russo," O'Shea greeted his fellow detective.

"Come on. I'll take you to the room."

The two men walked down the corridor before finally taking a right at the adjacent hallway.

How did it come to this? O'Shea wondered. There was a time when he was so proud to be a detective, the day he traded the squad car for his trusty El Camino. Now he was stuck with a chaperone. Nine months ago, he showed up at the station stinking like a distillery and vomited during a briefing. The Captain called it a mandatory leave of absence (which was a nice way of saying he'd been suspended). He started going to AA and returned to work once he was clean and sober. It went fine at first, but he got the rookie assignments. First a vandalism report, then a run of the mill break-in and now Russo's sloppy seconds.

Next they'll have me rescuing cats from trees.

"Is that the case file?" said O'Shea, motioning at the file folder.

Russo flinched. "Sorry, no. It's back at the station."

"Guess you had better fill me in then."

"We had a report of a possible two-forty. Victim was found—"

"Save the cop-talk, will you?" said O'Shea impatiently. "Just tell me what happened."

Russo sighed. "Far as we can tell, this guy was giving himself a little treat, if you know what I mean," he said with raised eyebrows. O'Shea grunted in acknowledgment. "Anyhow, something went wrong. Maybe somebody interrupted and beat the hell out of him, not really sure."

"What do you mean maybe?"

"There were no fingerprints, footprints, forced entry, nothing. He's only given me bits and pieces so far. What we need is a statement."

"Is he conscious?"

"Should be."

They passed a bank of elevators before arriving at a stark white room with six beds lined with curtains. A nurse sat next to the bed on the far side.

The patient was lying motionless on his back like a dead walrus, a series of tubes and IVs sticking out of his left arm. O'Shea stood in the doorway watching him as the EKG beeped with each beat of his pulse. He had very thin hair and a black goatee that had grown just a little too long. His left eye was swollen so badly it had become the size and color of a plum. His nose was bandaged, nostrils clotted with so much blood, each breath sounded like they were blocked by a piece of Lego.

The nurse left as soon as she knew the detectives were there.

"I'll leave you to it," said Russo as he turned to leave. "See you back at the station. You'll be okay?"

"Just dandy," said O'Shea as he entered the room.

The patient didn't even seem to notice as the detective took a seat where the nurse had been sitting moments ago. For a moment, O'Shea wasn't sure that he was in fact awake until he saw his eyes glued to the faded paint on the ceiling. Something told him that aside from Russo and the nurse, no one else had visited.

"Mister Kowalski," he said, "I'm Detective O'Shea. I'd like to ask you a few questions."

No answer. No sign at all that he had been heard or was even on the same planet as this man.

"Mister Kowalski?"

"Do you believe in God, Detective?" He spoke so suddenly it almost made O'Shea jerk.

The detective took a small pad and pen from his coat pocket. "In my line of work, it's pretty damn hard."

"I know what you mean. At least, I used to." His speech was lazy and slurred from what was undoubtedly a cocktail of painkillers.

"According to the report, you were found severely injured and unconscious after a nine-one-one call was made from your residence. During that call, you stated that you'd been attacked. Is that correct?"

"Yes."

"By whom?" he asked and began to scribble on his notepad.

"I—I don't know."

"You didn't see the culprit?"

Dennis shook his head.

"Is there anyone you can think of that might want to harm you physically, someone with a grudge or anything like that?"

"No one," Dennis answered shakily.

"I see," said O'Shea, trying to mask his skepticism. When it came to bullshit, Detective O'Shea had a particularly well-honed sense of smell.

"Is there anyone else who might have had a key to your apartment?"

Dennis shook his head again. "The only other person that had a key was my mother."

"And where was she at the time of the attack?" *Scribble, scribble.*

"Holy Cross Cemetery. She died four months ago."

"I'm sorry," said O'Shea as he scratched out what he had just written on his notepad. "How did she pass?"

"Heart attack. Sudden, but not her first. She'd been having health problems for a while."

"How come?" O'Shea asked. The question didn't have anything to do with the case. Asking questions, like listening, was simply part of being a detective. And they were both crucial to gaining a person's trust.

"Drinking, smoking, gambling, double bacon cheeseburgers, you name it. Then one day in June," Dennis lightly snapped his fingers, "gone. Finally caught up with her when she was playing the slots in Atlantic City. Momma loved the slots. She was very religious too. Went to church every Sunday without fail. But for all her praying, you'd think she could have tried taking a walk or eating a salad once in a while."

"You make it sound like she deserved it," said O'Shea.

"I'd never say a thing like that!" said Dennis angrily. "But I can't really say I was surprised. It was just a matter of time. Momma got to the point of needing a motorized cart just to get around. She was only fifty-seven, but the way she went on about it, you would have thought she was ninety-seven."

Detective O'Shea didn't know Dennis Kowalski, but already he knew what kind of man he was. He had met ones like him before. Despite his generous girth, he seemed so small, like he would give anything in the world to crawl into a hole and away from the eyes of the world.

"Did the two of you live together?" he asked, jotting things quickly across the pad as he thought of them.

Dennis nodded slowly, rolling his eyes as he did. "I know what you're thinking...lives with his mother, probably plays D&D and never been laid, right? But it's not like that. She needed help and I said I would move in. Simple as that."

With clear discomfort Dennis sat up in the hospital bed and folded his hands across his generous belly. "True, it wasn't always smooth sailing though. I mean, how could it be? She treated me like I was still ten-years-old. Always wanting to know where I was going, what I was doing, when I'd be home. One time she," he paused and cleared his throat, "caught me boinking the baloney when I thought she'd gone to bingo, and guilted me into confessing to her priest. Can you believe it? A grown man apologizing like a kid caught stealing candy."

"You could have said no," O'Shea said without looking up from his notes.

"I did at first. But she raved like a proper lunatic and swore that I'd burn in the fires of Hell. Personally, between Hell and her ranting, I'd rather burn. If it meant keeping her calm, if it meant keeping her quiet…"

"I see." O'Shea scribbled something down on his notepad—*Boinking the baloney*—so he could laugh about it later.

"I'm sorry if I seem a bit hesitant, but it was embarrassing."

"Of course." O'Shea looked up for the first time, wondering what this had to do with the assault. "I'm not here to judge, Mister Kowalski. Just tell me what happened."

He took a deep breath. "Why not…and you can call me Dennis."

"Dennis. Please continue."

"Momma left a little money behind, life insurance mostly, but she actually did pretty well at the slots over the years. She left half to her church and the other half to me. Not enough to retire on, but ten grand is still quite the windfall." Then, leaning a little closer, Dennis said, "May I confess something wicked, Detective?"

That got his attention, and O'Shea looked Dennis in his glassy blue eyes.

"Everything in that apartment was hers. The furniture, appliances, the TV, even the decoration was specifically insisted upon. There was barely a bare patch of wall not covered with a crucifix or a framed picture of Jesus. She even demanded I hang one above my bed because mine was the only room without. 'To keep the home holy,' she said. "I really wanted something of my own, something just for me that Momma would *never* have allowed. Not in a million years. I try to be kind, but honestly, Momma was difficult to live with. So I felt a little reward was called for. There's nothing wrong with that, is there?

"I thought about it for a while before finding the perfect thing. I had to order it from Germany and it took eight weeks to be custom-made and shipped. Cost the better part of the money, too.

"Finally, one day two burly men with shaved heads and neck tattoos showed up with a big wooden box. I opened it as soon as they left, and there she was. My very own Candi Cox doll."

Detective O'Shea stopped taking notes. He was just listening now. Dennis seemed like a kid describing the new bike he got for his birthday.

"I know that's a pretty weird thing to look forward to, but..."

"No need to explain, Dennis. Everyone has their little secret things," said O'Shea, thinking about the bottle of Jim Beam he used to keep in his desk drawer.

"Secret things," said Dennis enthusiastically. "Yes, exactly. See, you understand. I thought about taking a trip to Las Vegas for some, you know, company. But I've been there, done that. I've seen the faces of the girls when they're with me — like catching a strong whiff of garbage. They try, but still their faces wrinkle up when they do.

"Besides, this way I figured she wouldn't just be a lover, but a companion, too. She could fill the hole Momma left."

O'Shea squirmed in his seat.

"She looked like a droid in an escape pod the way she was sitting in the box. I gave her a nice warm bath to get rid of the sawdust and sterile factory smell she had.

"I picked up some clothes from Victoria's Secret earlier. Only the best for my girl," he said with a dizzy wink and a smile. "I wanted to mark the occasion, so I made smoked salmon with red potatoes and a bottle of Chianti. Normally I don't drink, but this was a special occasion.

"She looked stunning the way her blonde hair brushed the white satin of her nightgown like a wreath of gold. She was such a good listener, it was almost ten by the time I was finished talking. I had to admit, I was a little nervous. But already I felt a deep connection with her, like I could tell her anything in the world.

"I carried her to the bedroom like a groom taking his bride to the wedding bed. Her presence was so real in the dim orange glow of the candles around my bedroom — her black lashes, her emerald eyes, everything. My heart pounded as I shed my clothes and slid into her.

"And that's when I noticed something odd," said Dennis with a clear crack in his voice. "She was staring at me. Not up at the ceiling like she was just before, but right into my eyes. "Then…" Dennis let out several laughs of disbelief, "she smiled. I had to blink a few times to be sure, but it was true. And it wasn't a kind smile at all. It was evil. I tried to throw myself off her, but she was holding me back…by my *crotch*!"

O'Shea sucked air through his teeth as Dennis gripped his hair with two white-knuckled fists. "She slugged me when I tried to get free, but the more I fought the tighter she got until I was powerless against the pain!"

Dennis placed his face in his palms and sobbed quietly, his body jerking rapidly as if he had an acute case of hiccups. His cries grew louder, longer like an animal wounded in the woods. Despite Detective O'Shea's firm exterior, he couldn't help feeling sorry for the poor guy, this lonely man who was very clearly disturbed from a lifetime of invasion and mental oppression. He'd seen it more times than he could count.

Suddenly Dennis began to laugh. Softly at first, then louder.

He lifted his face from his hands, smiling. A crazed, mirthless rictus, twisted like a pipefitting about to burst, creased his chubby face. His bruised eyes had grown wide and lost in madness.

He took a very deep breath and howled at the top of his lungs: "SHE TOOK IT! SHE TOOK IT FROM ME! THAT BITCH! SHE TOOK IT TO PUNISH ME! HA HA HA!"

"Took what?" asked O'Shea as he watched Dennis slam his fist between his legs.

He can't mean…

"And why not? I can't have a normal life now. But I can have a righteous one. I can spread the word. I can warn others before it's too late for them."

Two orderlies rushed in just as Dennis sprung up on the bed, kneeling on it in a feeble attempt to peel the sweat-soaked hospital gown off his fat frame.

"Sorry, sir," said one of the orderlies as Detective O'Shea rose from his seat, "but you'll have to go now."

"That's alright," said O'Shea thankfully as he tucked his notepad back into his coat pocket. "I think I've got all I need."

He left the room quickly, pretending not to notice the bizarre outburst. As he waited for the elevator, he took one last look as Dennis let out a great wail of triumph. One of the men was trying in vain to secure his arms as the other prepared a syringe. His husky body was now naked, revealing the dark, swollen area between his legs where his genitals should have been.

When Detective O'Shea returned to the station, the elusive case file was waiting for him on his desk. It didn't matter much now since it was on the fast track to an open and shut case.

Nothing surprising medically — victim suffered mild shock as a result of blood loss. No transfusion required. No sign of narcotics or hallucinogens.

From the information Detective Russo had gathered so far, O'Shea began to get a rough picture of the events.

The "assault" occurred around 10:00 pm. A call was made to 911 at 10:28. A brief transcript followed which showed that the victim frantically told the operator he had been attacked, but made no mention of the attacker. He did say that he had hidden in the front hall closet where, it was assumed, he found the tools for a makeshift blowtorch. A can of hairspray and a barbecue lighter were found in the kitchen next to Dennis himself unconscious and bleeding with the phone off the hook.

The doll had been found face down in the middle of the hallway with her face half melted and hair burned. After it arrived at the lab, officers found Dennis Kowalski's bloody penis in the doll's mouth, by which time it was too late to re-attach.

There were several photos included. Three shots of the doll where she was found and a close-up of her mangled face. There were two shots of the victim's injuries, face and what was left of the groin. The last one stuck out from the others. It was a shot of the wall next to the doll's resting place where a single word had been sloppily scrawled in black melted silicone—SINNER.

His fingers found a post-it note stuck to the back of the folder with a pair of numbers he recognized immediately as evidence tag numbers. Either on a hunch, morbid curiosity or both, O'Shea decided to check this out himself, but he had a feeling he wouldn't need the tag numbers.

Upon entering the evidence room, he passed rows and rows of files, cardboard and plastic boxes, bicycles, and a rack of tagged rifles and shotguns until he came to a row of metal racks where everything from stolen TVs and sporting goods to Gucci purses were kept.

The doll lay on the bottom shelf like a corpse on a morgue slab which, had she been a real girl, is exactly where she would have been. Her head was turned just enough for the scorched side to face him, like she had been expecting him. O'Shea fixed this right away so that her blank doll's eyes pointed away from him. An acrid smell like burnt plastic filled his nostrils. He found nothing out of the ordinary except for some dried blood around the corner of the mouth.

He didn't know what to think.

The only logical conclusion was that Dennis Kowalski had inflicted this bizarrely sadistic act on himself. But then why were his hands not injured from punching his own face? Did he use something else? If so, what?

It was unlikely that a man could castrate himself with only his bare hands, and nothing about Dennis Kowalski said great strength, physical or otherwise. Then a knife or a pair of scissors would have been needed. But no such item was found at the scene. In fact, the medical report showed that the separation had been far too messy to indicate a sharp object.

But how else to explain it?

It would be unimaginably difficult for a person to do something like that to themselves. Not just because of the strength involved, but the pain.

The very thought of it made O'Shea uneasy. He decided to leave it alone for tonight. He was tired, hungry and longed for the sanctuary of his humble abode, empty as it was. When compared to the misfortune of others, suddenly his life didn't seem like such a pair of snake eyes. At least there was still the job. Thank god for that.

Detective O'Shea yawned and turned heel to leave.

Squeak.

It came from the metal racks as if they had been bumped ever so slightly, so sudden that he almost reached for his gun. When he spun around, nothing had stirred. But there was something odd about the doll, something out of place. He could have sworn that a split second ago, just for an instant, she was looking at him.

ACTS OF VIOLENCE

The idea behind this one was pretty simple: there are lots of horror stories involving a possessed doll of some kind. I thought, what if it was a sex doll? That's pretty much it. And since this was one of the first stories I wrote after getting sober, that's something I worked into the story.

UNDER THE BLACK TOP

"I THOUGHT WE WERE GOING TO THE CARNIVAL," LILY whined as children do.

"We are," Rachel said, not even looking up from her phone as they crossed the street. "We're meeting Kathy and Jason."

"Why?"

Rachel looked at her daughter, raising her eyebrows. "Because they're coming with us."

Lily huffed. "I'd rather go alone."

Yeah, well I'd rather not go at all, but here we are. The words came so near to escaping her lips that she could taste them, mingled with the hint of her last afternoon sangria at the back of her throat.

Rachel's usual attire—what had become her usual attire since her divorce—of a baggy hoodie, sweat pants with frazzled hair and resting mom face was gone at least. Replaced with a simple but cute V-neck. Auburn hair shaken out to give a bit more body. She had even put on makeup, a rarity nowadays.

Lily, on the other hand, looked her usual self. Dressed in a pair of overalls, gingery brown hair scrunched up in a ponytail, clinging to her stuffed dog Scrappy though she was far too old to take it with her wherever she went. But that didn't stop her. Rachel didn't make much of a fuss about it. Scrappy was like her security blanket and figured she had to grow out of carrying him around eventually.

It was a beautifully warm evening, barely a cloud in the sky. As they reached the park, Rachel watched her daughter run off into the lush green grass, her brown hair flying behind her.

Lily ran toward the jungle gym, lost in her own world. Beyond it lay a thin but expansive patch of Illinois woods where people biked along the trails and old couples walked their dogs.

There by the swings Rachel saw a blonde woman and a young boy playing on the see-saw. They stopped tilting back and forth as Lily reached them and stood up.

The woman waved at her.

A swarm of butterflies fluttered up through her stomach as Rachel managed to wave back. It was Kathy, her neighbor and friend, with her son Jason who was the same age as Lily.

The two women came face-to-face and exchanged smiles. Although Kathy was a few years older, in her mid-thirties, they got along like old high school friends.

"Okay, can we go now?" Lily asked, begging with her bright green eyes. Rachel weakened every time she saw them.

"In a minute. Why don't you go play for a bit?"

"But it's getting late." Another whine.

"And the carnival's not going anywhere. Go play hide and seek or something."

"Yeah yeah yeah," Jason excitedly chimed in agreement.

Both women looked at each other, exchanging glances in silent motherly communication.

"Fine," Lily huffed.

The kids tore off into the woods. Rachel and Kathy took a seat on a nearby bench.

"So, how are you doing?" Kathy asked in that half sympathetic, half pitying way of hers.

Rachel shrugged and folded her arms. "Same old..." she sighed. "You?"

"Ugh," Kathy answered, rolling her eyebrows. "Colin's been driving me nuts." She gave her hair a flip and with it the smell of coconut all but pulled her an inch or two closer.

Rachel leaned back in her seat. "Yeah, husbands will do that."

Three months, Rachel thought. *It's been three months.* Every day of it crawled by, and yet it seemed like no time at all.

"No no, I don't mean it like that," Kathy replied with an intake of breath. "Just listen to this. You won't believe it." She straightened up to prepare for her story.

Rachel heard very little of it. Something about Colin's friend dying in Australia in a surfing accident.

"Oh my god," Rachel replied quietly, half-heartedly. She couldn't stop thinking about how pretty Kathy was. With her soft blonde hair and bright eyes, smooth skin and the figure of a personal trainer even after having a kid—something she envied. *I can see why he was attracted to her,* she thought.

"Yeah, he was a great guy," Kathy said remorsefully. "Could make you laugh no matter what. So ever since they were teenagers, he and Colin talked about buying a boat so they could sail around the world. And now that's what he wants to do...buy a boat!"

"Oh great," she scoffed. "Does he want to sail around the world too?"

"I sure hope not," said Kathy. "I mean, we could afford it. But where the hell is there to sail around here? The damn thing would probably just end up an eyesore sitting in our backyard forever like a tornado had blown it there."

They each had a good laugh at that.

"So, how's Lily doing with...you know...everything?"

Rachel didn't answer nor acknowledge the question at first. She just stared into space. Nervous.

"Not so good," Rachel said finally. "Keeps asking why Rick had to leave…"

"You haven't told her why I take it." Oh, she was good. She was very good. The tone in her voice was sincere but for all the wrong reasons. It almost convinced her.

"No," Rachel simply replied.

"So what do you tell her?"

What should I tell her? That you were fucking him and probably still are? That I've smelled you on our sheets and both loved and hated it? That I wish it was me *you were sleeping with instead? All those nights of talking, drinking wine, sharing things, was that nothing to you? That every time you call me sweetie, I melt? Is that what I should tell her?*

Rachel sighed as she balled her fingers up in the palm of her hand, wincing just a little with the sound of the cracks they made. "That Mommy and Daddy don't love each other anymore, but that we still love her with all our hearts."

Rachel paused. Desolate.

"And then, when she'd ask why we didn't love each other, all I could think to say is that that's what happens to grown-ups sometimes. It's too hard to explain. Even to myself."

Kathy put her arm around Rachel's shoulder to comfort her and she broke all the way down.

"I never wanted this."

"Of course you didn't."

"I'm just so confused and don't know how to fix…anything."

"I know, sweetie," Kathy answered. Just her being there made things seem better.

Sweetie. Lost completely now, Rachel saw through her eyes but couldn't seem to control herself. She looked dead ahead at the wind in the grass for what felt like forever before turning her head upward, aiming her lips toward Kathy's.

Kathy stood and backed away as if she'd just pulled a knife on her. The look on her face was of utter surprise. Confusion. Disgust.

"I-I..." Rachel stammered. She shook her head and nervously smiled.

I'm not sorry.

"Found you!" Lily shouted. Jason was tucked in, arms folded over his knees, to a small pocket of brush.

They giggled together as a flock of crows flapped their wings and flew from the branches of the trees above.

"Okay," Jason said with a smile. "Now you go hide and I'll find you." Lily took off as Jason started counting. "Thirty, twenty-nine, twenty-eight..."

The foliage became a green blur as she rushed over a weed-covered knoll and down a hill. A dirt path ran along the bottom, her feet smacked away from where he was and then to a small hollow just below, right near the creek.

Lily wondered where to hide. Behind the maple tree? No, no good. In the little dip by the bridge, covered up with leaves? No, there were bugs and stuff in there.

Then like the caress of a gentle breeze, she heard music. Very soft and tranquil it found her and she slowly started walking off to her right. It was like perfume, this music. Sweet and strong, drawing her forward. The notes bobbing up and down like horses on a merry-go-round.

Do-DOO-DOO, Do-DOO-DOO, Do-DOO-DOO. Do-DOO-DOO, Do-DOO-DOO, Do-DOO-DOO.

And then, by the bank of the creek, she saw where it was coming from. An old man sat on a large moss-covered rock playing a wooden flute. Dressed in old dirty clothes, his shoes were brown and caked with mud and a wide-brimmed hat adorned his brow, white wisps of hair poking out from under. He looked like an old farmer.

Lily approached and as she did the old man continued to play his song. The notes brushing her ears like the touch of a feather. She stood right next to him.

Holding the flute in both hands, the man moved it from his mouth and then looked at her slowly.

With the music still in her head, Lily smiled at him accompanied by the frothy flow of the babbling creek.

He smiled back a crooked brown clash of teeth. "Hello, child."

Lily was unafraid though the old man's face was wrinkled and gray. A faint bit of white stubble about his cheeks and chin. But his eyes were an unusual blue, almost sparkling with the orange light of dusk playing off the clear waters of the creek.

"Hello."

"And what's your name?" There was an accent in his words, close to her piano teacher Mr. Kaufman.

"Lily," she answered. "What's yours?"

"My name is Gaspar," he answered with a flick of his eyebrows. "Would you like to see a trick?"

"Sure," Lily answered. The old man raised his chin and shut his eyes, making a circular gesture with his hands. Putting the right arm in his lap, the left hand sprung forward toward Lily's face. He snapped, and at the tip of his thumb a flame appeared.

Lily flashed a toothy, white grin. "Ha! That's cool. How did you do that?"

"Magic, my dear," the old man replied. "Care to see another?"

Before Lily could say yes, the old man made a similar, sinewy motion with his hands. Before her eyes, a mass of orange fur appeared in the old man's grasp.

A precious, marmalade kitten peered at her with beautifully green eyes. He handed it to Lily and she cuddled it against her cheeks as the tiny thing purred.

"Can I keep her?"

"She's yours," the old man smiled. His teeth made Lily wince a little. But as soon as the kitten stretched out her soft paw and brushed her nose, she was hooked.

She had always wanted an orange kitten. Thoughts spilled through her head of afternoons in the sun watching her pounce at butterflies in the backyard garden and cuddling up with her as they both took a lazy Sunday nap, the lovely sound of purring lulling her to sleep.

Something broke her from the dream. The crush of dried sticks and leaves sounded over the bubbling of the creek, a little louder with each step. Then in the distance, a blonde tuft of hair bobbed between the branches of the bushes next to the path above. It was Jason. And he hadn't spotted her yet.

"I have to go now," Lily whispered very gently to the old man.

"Go where?"

"I have to hide."

The old man leaned in close and whispered back, "I have the perfect place for you to hide, sweet child."

"Where?"

"Somewhere where you'll *never* be found." He stretched out his wrinkled, gray hand. "I promise…"

"That would be great…if I wanted to get murdered!"

Gaspar said nothing, completely taken aback.

"Yeah," said Lily, "I'm ten, not stupid. Later, weirdo."

She went to leave but didn't get more than a step before his hand was on her wrist.

Tight.

And with it came the sound of a calliope, the smell of cotton candy and popcorn…

"Jason!" Kathy called out, frustration in her voice.

"Kath, wait," Rachel called after her. "Can't we just talk—"

"There's nothing to talk about."

The final shards of purple dusk splintered through the dark

silhouette of maple trees as the two women approached the border of the woods.

"Lil!," Rachel called. "Lily?"

The wind grew stronger, and when there was no answer from the woods, Kathy began to call for Jason. Then a few yards away a small figure appeared from the path between the trees.

"I'm here, Mom."

The two mothers stepped quickly over to where the voice came from. "Jason," said Kathy, relieved. "Where's Lily?"

"I don't know."

"What do you mean you don't know?" asked Rachel, a slight crack in her voice.

"She went to hide a while ago and I never found her. Then it got darker out and I heard you calling."

Rachel went completely silent. Still. Her arms wrapped around her chest to shield herself from the wind.

"Lily!" Rachel bellowed firmly over the wind, hoping she would be heard.

Then without saying a word she ran off down the path calling out her daughter's name at the top of her lungs. She wasn't fully alarmed just yet, though truthfully she felt the grip of fear the second the words *I don't know* were uttered. The perpetually inherent worry every mother felt every second of every day was telling her something was off.

No, everything's okay, Rachel thought. *She's just wandered off somewhere where she can't hear me.*

...

But what if she wasn't?

It was dark out now. What if she had fallen face down in the creek or been attacked by a coyote or something?

"Oh God!" Rachel cried aloud.

She ran. As if it were to save her own life, because in many ways it was. Without Lily, she was all alone. The sound of her heart thundered in her ears louder than the thrash of bush branches against her body. Louder than the stamping of her feet. Louder than her own harrowed screams calling her name. And in her mind she saw the face of her daughter crying for her, begging for her to come find her and take her home and make everything okay again.

Rachel finally reached the hill and skidded down as fast as possible without taking a tumble. It was so dark now all she could make out was the canopy of maple trees clawing at the navy blue horizon and the ghostly reflection of distant light on the creek. How could she ever hope to find her daughter in this?

If only she had a flashlight or even a lighter. She could set some dried leaves on fire maybe. She didn't care. If there was a chance Lily would see it…

"*LILY?*" she screamed so hard it made her cough. "*LILY, WHERE ARE YOU?*" Rachel lost her composure as her face shrunk to a horribly wrinkled mask of horror and the tears flowed as if bleeding. Losing a child was every parent's worst nightmare. But this was no bad dream. She was living it.

Her breath began to hitch, sending a storm of sharp air through her chest.

All thought, all other emotions save for panic, were stripped away and left a desperate raving woman staggering blindly through the darkened woods. Further and further Rachel wandered through the blackness. With nothing else to do, she then strayed from the path. Very near the bank of the creek her ankle buckled, causing her to fall shoulder-first into the frigid water. A flat pain filled her entire left side as it struck the rocks of the creek bed beneath her.

Weeping desperately and drenched from head to hip, her shoulder throbbed as her swollen hand made contact with the ground.

Rachel grabbed hold of something as she crawled gingerly to her feet. Soft and cold and caked with mud, but it felt familiar.

When she held it up against the contrast of the sky, there was no mistake.

A light. Behind her a spark pierced through the gloom, bobbing back and forth as it neared. Rachel heard her name being called from the same direction. It was Kathy running down the path with a flashlight in hand.

She found Kathy finally as the yellow circle of light settled on her; dazed and vacant, she held her daughter's toy puppy in one trembling hand.

Even before she saw the girl, there was the smell of cotton candy. Spinning lights. The rush of a rollercoaster. People screaming. But not in fear. In joy. Excitement. The unbridled thrill of danger and adrenaline made vocal. She stood with her back to her, perfectly still. Silhouetted against the strobing, zoetropic effect of the merry-go-round ahead. It spliced each motion, no matter how small, frame by frame until she was facing her.

And just like that, the distance closed between them as if the space had simply melted away.

Her brown hair hung loose at her shoulders, thick with clumps of dirt. The skin had greyed to a point of death and the whites of her eyes had overtaken the entirety of both sockets.

Her face, twisted and anguished and reddened so the tears that streamed down her cheeks appeared as blood, yawned open so that the jaw hung slack.

"I thought we were going to the carnival..."

Her hand shot up and grabbed at her.

Rachel screamed her daughter's name as she awoke from the nightmare to the cold sting of reality.

It was midnight and the house was quiet, barren as a desert moon.

A month had passed without any sign of her girl. Thirty-three days, to be exact. Thirty-three days of missing child reports, visits from the local police, social services, outreach groups, support groups and Rachel's former in-laws who practically beat down the door to tell her what a bad mother she was for losing their granddaughter while she curled into a ball on the other side of it.

Extensive searches of the woods where she had disappeared had been conducted, including a human chain complete with dogs to sniff out any trace of her using Scrappy to get the scent, fittingly enough. Not so much as an extra footprint had been found. It was as if she had simply disappeared into thin air.

Rick had blamed her of course, said if she hadn't let Lily go wandering off she would still be with them. He had always been over-protective but never a bastard with the gall to say something so cruel at such a time.

But at least he wouldn't have lost her.

Rachel smoked cigarettes, something she had never done before except for once back in high school. Her afternoon sangria was replaced with all-day vodkas, and the empty bottles outnumbered the milk cartons. All bearing her Lily's face.

HAVE YOU SEEN ME? they pleaded and taunted every time she opened the refrigerator, spilling more words out. **NO OF COURSE YOU HAVEN'T. YOU WERE TOO BUSY OGLING SOME BLONDE PIECE OF ASS WHO WILL NEVER FEEL THE SAME WAY ABOUT YOU. OH WELL. DON'T FORGET TO DRINK YOUR MILK BEFORE I GO SOUR...LIKE MY BODY PROBABLY IS IN A SHALLOW GRAVE SOMEWHERE.**

She went on solitary walks to the park, even when it rained, which seemed to be all too often lately. Like tonight. She could hear the drops patter against the windows, watering her sorrow like a houseplant.

Rachel rose from the tangled sheets of her bed, threw on her housecoat and stumbled downstairs. A bottle of Absolut lay on the floor at the bottom. As if it had slipped right out of her hand as she climbed the stairs to bed. She didn't even remember leaving it there. She gave it a jiggle. Just enough to splash around inside. She uncapped it and swigged a small mouthful, draining it. Then dropped it pretty much right back where she had found it.

Aside from the glow of street lamps outside, casting scarce squares of yellow light through the rain-covered living room windows, the house was completely dark. She left it that way. Rachel lumbered over to the sofa and collapsed on her side, staring at the awkward shadows spread across the floor.

She couldn't bear to stay in this house. Couldn't stand to linger in the doorway of Lily's room, paralyzed with grief, murmuring to herself the songs they used to sing together from the Disney films they loved so much. But she couldn't bear to leave it.

What if Lily came back? There's still a chance…right? If only she would. If she could just magically show up on her doorstep right now, she'd happily take her to a carnival. They'd hit the road and find every carnival and county fair in the state, in the Midwest, in the country if that's what it took to have her baby back.

Rachel couldn't bring herself to look at pictures of her anymore. When she did she couldn't stop. What had once brought a smile to her face had become salt in her wounds. And it was then that she realized that there would never be any more. None of graduation or wedding photos, not even another birthday would be captured forever on paper or pixels. The grief welled up inside her and finally spilled over.

And it's my fault, she thought. *It's all my fault*.

There was no thought of ending her life. It wasn't so linear as that any more than we think about scratching an itch or picking a scab. It was reflexive. Innate. A conclusion that had been building for a while now.

All at once Rachel rose from the sofa and went into the

kitchen. She stood over the sink, tracing the contour of the stainless steel with her eyes, thinking it could use a splash of color. Red perhaps. Yes, red would do nicely.

Her hand went to the nearby block of knives and drew one. Perfect for slicing, dicing and paring, though she doubted KitchenAid had wrists in mind when they made it. Gripping the handle tight in one hand and turning the other skyward, she bent her elbow back for a moment and closed her eyes.

There was a knock at the front door. Three in fact, loud and clear.

She dropped the knife clattering into the kitchen sink and practically leapt from the spot. Bare footsteps squeaked on the linoleum floor as they put her where she needed to be. It wouldn't be her, of course. It couldn't be. Even though that was immediately where her mind went. But a police officer. A neighbor. Someone with some kind of news.

Oh god…but what *news?*

Rachel unlocked the door and flung it open.

There, standing on the porch, was her daughter. Dressed in exactly the same clothes she had been wearing that day, skin coated in a glossy sheen of rain from head to toe, trembling as the rain pummeled her. Her hair hung soaked and ragged in front of her face like strands of wet rope. Aside from her shakes, Lily didn't move.

A moment passed between them. Rachel looked harder at the girl. Her green eyes seemed duller somehow. Hair darkened by the rain. Skin drained of color to an almost pale grey complexion.

Dozens of times since she had gone missing, Rachel had seen Lily holding someone else's hand in the supermarket or through the window of a school bus as it sped by on the street. But never like this.

"Mommy," she croaked finally, her lips quivering, eyes wild and crazed.

Rachel's composure sunk to a fit of whimpering as she fell to her knees and wrapped her arms tight around Lily. Embraced her with complete abandon, instantly gathered her up as if she were small again and brought her into the house. She took off her housecoat and covered Lily with it.

"Baby," Rachel sniffled, cradling her head against her shoulder. "Baby, where have you been?"

She repeated the question over and over, her own voice the only tether to her frayed and faltering sanity.

Finally she pried her face away from her daughter's and looked at it.

Vacant as the Bates Motel. Eyes open but looking at nothing. Seeing nothing.

"Stay right here, okay?" said Rachel. "I'll be right back."

Back into the kitchen she went, feet squeaking more than before thanks to the rain. Her hands were shaking as she reached out for the phone on the counter.

Do I call the police? Or 911? If this isn't an emergency, what is?

Her thoughts raced—the tiniest little *tink* of metal from behind her, but thought nothing of it—as she plucked the receiver and pounded on the buttons.

A knife buried itself in the phone, narrowly missing her fingers.

Rachel screamed and jumped back in horror.

Lily held the very knife she had been holding just a few minutes ago, having jabbed it into the phone like a stake into a vampire's heart. Her gaze fixed on the split piece of plastic, then twisted hard toward her.

"You weren't there!" Lily rasped, teeth clenched. Baring them like a rabid dog.

Rachel began to hyperventilate, breathing one hard, broken breath after another. Repulsed, shocked by the thing before her. For surely this was not her daughter.

"YOU WEREN'T THERE!"

Rachel bolted from the spot.

Lily was on her right away. Leapt onto her back, wrapped her arm around her mother's throat and began to squeeze.

Rachel threw herself backwards into the kitchen wall, knocking the wind out of Lily as she fell off her, crumbling to the ground. Without hesitating, she ran for her life. Flying up the stairs as fast as she could, into her bedroom and locked it.

Moments passed. Long, ugly moments eager to catch up with her. They formed themselves into a silence. And the silence became a hope.

Hope that she was gone. That whoever or whatever it was that looked like her daughter had left the house and wouldn't return.

But it was too good to be true.

The hushed but tell-tale sound of footsteps crept along the carpeted floor outside her bedroom door. The little sliver of light beneath it broke as a shadow appeared in it.

No sound.

Then the metallic scratch of something hard and sharp being dragged across it from the other side.

Something hit hard.

Rachel's breaths burned in her throat.

Then another. It was faint, but she heard the very slightest splintering of wood.

Retreating to the bathroom, Rachel slammed the door shut as a third hit turned that splinter into a definite crack.

She went to lock the door…only it didn't lock. One of the many things Rick was supposed to have fixed long ago. There was still a solid memory of him saying that he was going to the hardware store to get what he needed to repair it, but never did. Probably because he was off fucking Kathy instead.

Rachel looked frantically around for something to defend herself with. She yanked open a bathroom drawer, rummaging around inside it to no avail.

The bedroom door finally gave way, breaking free of the frame and slamming hard into the wall behind it right outside.

She looked in another drawer, this one nearest to the bathroom door, and pulled up a pair of scissors. Glistening and sharp. Clutched tight in one hand like a dagger, she hid behind the door just as the knob began to twist. Slow and tight like a screw digging its way into her heart.

All at once the door was forced open with a *bang*.

Rachel stabbed downward with the scissors. A reflex. Expecting that they would be buried in the neck of a ten-year-old girl.

Instead piercing nothing but air.

The door hit the last drawer she left open, unable to go further.

It was pulled back and slammed again and again into it, trying to break the obstruction to no avail. Rick may not have repaired the lock, but whoever had installed their bathroom drawers sure knew what they were doing.

A hand shot through, and with it, the kitchen knife it held. Flailing about wildly, curving behind the door to see if a cut could be made. Trying to stab any bit of her it could get, but she was safely out of reach.

Ironic. A few minutes ago she was about to cut herself with that very knife.

The knife and the fist that held it retracted back through the small opening with a couple of clumsy scrapes.

Why didn't I kick the door closed on her arm? I should have. Why didn't I? Stupid.

She stood at such an angle that Rachel was able to see through the narrow amount of space left between the door and the frame in the bathroom mirror.

A wide and waiting eye peered through, piercing her in a way the knife couldn't. If a look could cut.

The mouth beneath it smiled a broken smile. No joy or warmth in it. Only malice.

"His name was Gaspar," Lily spoke. Low and hushed, but

perfectly clear. "Papa Gaspar. Best showman this side of the River Styx. And he loves children. *His* children. His totenkinder."

Lily left the door just long enough to pull a chair up to the door and got comfy.

"I tried to run, but he took me by the wrist and suddenly we were in a deep black forest. Nothing but gnarled trees clawing at the blanched sky above.

"The sound of circus music wound its way through the path guiding us away from the trees. Calling me.

"Suddenly his grip wasn't so tight on me anymore. Instead I found myself holding his hand. Letting him lead me as our footsteps crunched through leaves on the ground like dry brittle bones. His clothes had changed too. Now he wore a red tailcoat tight against his tall, skeletal frame. Hand clutched upon a cane with a top hat perched upon his head. He looked far less sickly in that woods, where color dared not tread. His face marvelously pale and gaunt.

"Through the thick cluster of dead trees it opened up to a field. Bright but faded. And yet there was no sun. No shadow. Just a cloudless expanse of gray sky. Blinding. Everything leeched of its color.

"Ahead were all manner of carnival attractions. The Ferris wheel I saw first, spinning languidly like a giant pinwheel. Then a carousel. A funhouse. And games! Lots of games. But they were all empty. And in the distance a tent. A marquee, black as sackcloth. Standing crooked upon a knoll of dead grass overlooking it all. Taller than it was wide. A flag flapping at the top though there was no wind.

" 'Come child,' he spoke as we drew nearer to it.

" 'What will I see?'

" 'The greatest show not of this earth.'

"He pulled back the curtain…

"I don't even remember stepping inside. All of a sudden we were beneath a massive canopy, larger than it appeared from the outside by far.

"Here was the color missing from outside. Bright and vibrant. The inner part of the tent a deep crimson, almost purple where the shadows were deepest. Lit by blazing orange torchlight with flames roaring in iron braziers around the ring. The ground was packed with shallow light-colored sand and an odd copper twinge clung to the air.

"Papa Gaspar led me to a seat in the front row as he joined the procession.

"A band played a disjointed little tune while an organist cradled within the stands fondled the ivories.

"There were jugglers and men on stilts. Fire-eaters and sword swallowers. Contortionists, fat ladies, bearded ladies, painted ladies and dwarves. Clowns handing out balloons with great big lidless eyes in the center. Big cats, almost like shaved lions, no fur, just pale wrinkled skin. And elephants! The darkest of greys, almost black with morose red eyes. All marching in a circle.

"At the crack of a whip the procession parted as the ringleader stood center ring and the show started.

" 'Boys and girls, welcome to Papa Gaspar's Mitternachtszirkus. Where we delight the eye, dazzle the senses, and tempt your darker nature.

" 'I can see you all looking a bit nervous. But I assure you, while some may have reason to fear under the black top, you, boys and girls, are not the ones who should be afraid.'

"Horns blew and a set of large heavy wooden doors were opened.

"A line of people appeared. Some tall, some short. The short ones were children. At least, they looked like children. The tall ones were all grown-ups. Naked and downtrodden. Their necks and wrists shackled, attached to thick chains held by the ones who led them, lined them up and forced them to their knees.

" 'Here we have the very worst of the worst. Grown-ups who tell you that you are naughty for making a fuss or causing a spill. For refusing to go to bed on time. But as it turns out, grown-ups can be far naughtier than anything you could possibly imagine. Here we have the indifferent. The uncaring. The unwise. The insulting.'

"He came to an old man with a cross branded into his chest.

" 'The predatory.'

"The rest of the troupe began handing out a variety of objects. Bats, clubs, spikes, all manner of pain-inflicting instruments.

" 'Well, not under my roof. Here none of you will be grounded, spanked, chastised or preyed upon. Here, the grown-ups will learn the meaning of the word punishment.'

"He took out his whip, let one good hard crack of it go against their backs, and before the pain could even show in their faces, the children were upon them. Beating them over and over and over again until Papa let out another crack of the whip and they lay bloodied and sobbing in the center ring."

At this, Rachel's eyes were wide and watering. Hand over her mouth. Shaking.

"And that wasn't all. Oh no! For they were not dead.

"They were torn apart, limb from limb, by the elephants. Put in cages with the dread cats. Forced to jump through fiery rings only to be pulled down by Papa's whip and burned alive. Sawed in half...for real...when he did his magic show. Used by the clowns in their foolery as they juggled their internal organs. One came up to me and said, 'Lemme give ya a hand,' and thrust a severed one toward me.

"And you know what?"

Lily began to shake all over.

"I laughed! I enjoyed it. Every minute of it. Every tortured scream. Each warm spray of blood across my face.

"But even *that* wasn't the end for them. No. At first I thought it was just a trick of the light, the surrounding flames playing off the dark of their dead open eyes. But they weren't dead. Decapitated, dismembered, in some cases decimated. But not dead.

"Their mouths still choked, gasping for air. Twitching fingers still moved, trying to crawl away like crabs. In some cases a torso severed midway attempting to pull its way free to escape, leaving long bloody trails on the floor behind them. But before they could get too far they were gathered up by the tots who had led them out. Thrown into buckets. Collected to be sewn back together and used in the circus again and again and again. With not even death as a comfort."

The soft patter of many feet entered the bedroom. Padding into the room behind Lily until it was filled with little grey faces, punctuated by white eyes.

"I'm going to take you, Mommy. Like I was taken. You'll be part of the show now. And the show must go on."

"The show must go on…"

They all started in broken whispers, scattered like ripples on water.

"…The show must go on…"

A shadow appeared, stretched long and slender across the floor. Boxed at the head like a top hat. It made no sound. None at all.

"…The show must go on."

And as it moved nearer, covering her daughter entirely, turning her eyes to the same milky white as the other tots, Rachel couldn't help wishing with all her broken heart that she had just taken her daughter to the carnival.

This one was written at two different times. The first half under the title "Lollygagger" (not sure why, I just liked the word) but with no real plan in mind for it, it sat unfinished. Fast forward a few years when there was a submission call for a carnival horror anthology called Welcome to the Funhouse *and viola! That's what it became. It also turned into something of a cautionary tale, though why I can't really say for sure. On the surface it appears to caution parents who don't pay close enough attention to their kids, but really it's more about cautioning grown-ups not to lose sight of their inner child. That's how you wind up dead while still alive.*

SLASHER

Tonight was the night.

Five girls—five friends—had died by his hand. The Sitter Slasher, the papers had called him. (They had started with the full "Babysitter Slasher", but it was shortened before too long.)

And rightly so.

Were it not for his untimely capture and incarceration, he'd be well into the double digits by now. Four long years he had spent in a thirteen-by-seven cell awaiting the electric chair. And had it not been for the power outage the night he was set to be fried, that's just what would have happened. His escape was sweet, but not as sweet as his return.

And tonight he would make it six. Oh, how he had been waiting for this.

He watched her through the window, the girl. The future number six. He had only seen her for the first time earlier today at the mall and followed her home to this house. A sorority house, no less.

Perfect.

Its Greek letters adorned the threshold trellis of the house. He had no clue what they meant. To him, they meant a victim. A few lights were on. Not so much as to be obvious but enough to see that someone was home. It was surrounded by bushes; some latticed, some not. Somewhere in the distance, a dog barked.

Hidden and safe in the night. Nothing but the chirp of crickets to keep him company. Clothed completely in black. Nice and lean. A simple ski mask covering his face. No gimmick for him, those guys always got it in the end. Too many of his fellow slashers had already met their untimely fate—Denver Dodd, the Cincinnati Strangler, Chuckles the Killer Klown, Pigeon Man. All dead. No sequels for them.

Not him, though. He was in this for the long game. A career killer. He avoided the classic blunder of returning to the same town. Instead of going back for revenge, he went far away. Clear across the country to California.

Worth it. First I'll warm up a little here with Ms. Six. Then Seven, Eight, and Nine. Maybe when it's time for the big 1-0, I can return for sweet revenge.

The Slasher's hand gently stroked the handle of the hunting knife at his side. Sharp and lethal. Pining to pierce flesh.

There was that one perfect moment in time just before the tip gave way to a defenseless opening in the skin. Lush and warm.

Then red as could possibly be. Shades of red most people don't even know exist. *Deep* red.

Like her hair. Actually, it was more of a gingery orange really but definitely a redhead, the future Ms. Six. Athletic. Wearing a simple white cotton varsity sweater, no doubt representing her sorority. Cut off jean shorts and tennis shoes. Nothing out of the ordinary. And yet perfect. She yapped away on the kitchen phone to one of her friends, the sound of her voice audible but unclear.

Oblivious.

He didn't even know her name. Normally he preferred to know, but for his first time out in four years he would have to settle for Ms. Six. Besides, it didn't keep him from fantasizing about everything he was going to do to her. The touch and feel of every contour of her body as it lay bound and powerless beneath him. What her insides looked like. How hot she would look with her naked skin awash in the red of her own blood. How nice her head would look mounted on his wall with the others; though… those must have been confiscated by the police. Oh well. Time to start over.

And the cherry on top—his calling card. On each of his victims he left a handwritten note with the same nursery rhyme.

Little Miss Muffet sat on her tuffet, eating her curds and whey. When along came a spider who sat down beside her and frightened Miss Muffet away.

He had the note written and ready to go, folded in two in the cargo pocket of his pants. Feeling the glide of the pen on paper as he wrote it sent a pleasurable wave of anticipation through him he'd not known for too long. It was like revisiting an old friend. Oh, to leave it on a lifeless corpse again finally. Then they'd know —they'd all know—the Sitter Slasher was back!

He took out the cellular phone he had stolen earlier. A clunky thing but necessary tonight. It rang as soon as he finished dialing. And as it did the girl said something he couldn't make out but knew nevertheless—hang on, there's a call on the other line.

"Hello?"

"Hello."

"Hi, who's this?"

"Who do you want it to be?"

She gave her hair a flip. *"Well, I really want it to be my boyfriend."*

"I'm afraid I took care of him already," he lied. Didn't know she even had a boyfriend until now.

"Oh yeah? What did you do to him, huh? Chop him up? Slice him and dice him?"

"Uh…yeah." This was different. He expected something along

the lines of "You better cut it out, creep," or "The police are on their way." Or the ever-popular and direct but in every way futile, "What do you want?"

"Oh, you'll find out. Soon enough and in every way," he would say and let the moment linger a bit.

"Brad?" Or whatever his name would be.

"I told you. I'm not Brad."

Then something like that. But if he didn't know better, he'd say she was enjoying this.

Interesting.

"Yeah, that's just what I did," he answered finally.

"Don't spare the details. Spill it. What did you do to him, huh?"

"I cut off his head and threw it in the lake."

"That's so hot. Keep going."

"Then I…"

She wasn't moving. He knew full well that the best place to get in was right where he was standing—watching her through the kitchen window by the porch door. It would most likely have a decent lock, most glass doors do. But the one leading straight into the kitchen—the one she stood directly on the other side of yapping on the phone—looked far weaker. More compliant.

Normally once the phone call had been made they got nervous. Twitchy. Scared. They started moving around from window to window, looking out into the night before eventually getting completely away from them and holing up in one room or another clutching a sharp object like they knew how to use it. But not this girl. This one's thighs were practically steaming.

Well, they won't be in a second.

The Slasher moved around to the front of the house, careful not to disturb the bushes or bump into a garden gnome or something. Nothing that made a sound.

Prison keeps a man on his toes. Most of your day you spend dodging either a shiv or a shaft. Something another inmate wants to stick in you one way or another. And then there's the guards.

Most of them were just looking for a reason to give him a taste of their clubs, followed by a mouthful of his own blood. The lucky few that weren't a problem didn't care either way. Even so, he was pleased to see that even after years in the slammer he hadn't lost his touch.

After he made his move it would make her go toward the back door. Then he'd make his presence known at the back making her feel trapped, forcing her one of two ways—upstairs or down into the basement. Either way, he could deal with her. As long as he remembered to cut the phone line before she did.

He crept up onto the front porch, cast in the light of it for a brief moment, and went to the door.

He rang the doorbell. The classic *ding dong* sounded inside.

Anyone in their right mind would jump and reflexively start moving as far away from the thing that made a sudden noise in the night. Instead, Ms. Six made a line straight toward it. Stepping briskly toward the door instead of away from it.

Oh shit.

The Slasher dove over the railing and pressed his back up against the side of the house just as she strode out onto the porch.

"*So you wanna play hide and seek, huh?*" he heard, both through the phone and from her own lips less than ten feet away.

She went back inside and closed the door. As she did, the Slasher moved from his spot back to the cover of the bushes and tracked her through the living room window.

"*Or would you rather tell me some more about what you did to my beau?*"

"I chopped him up."

"*Uh-huh.*"

"Into little pieces."

"*Go on.*" Her hand dipped down between her legs.

"Then I put the pieces in a wood-chipper and sprayed bloody pulp all over the place."

"Oh yeah," she moaned. "That's it, big boy. I'm on fire. Now, why don't you come on in here and gimme some of that double penetration action?"

"What?"

"You heard me. Come on out from those bushes and stick me with everything you've got." She looked right at him. "I dare you."

OK. Not so oblivious.

This had never happened before. Clearly, Ms. Six was no ordinary bimbo. This one had spirit. Fire, even. He hated that. If they had that, they weren't afraid. And if they weren't afraid, he wasn't satisfied.

Well two can play that game, bitch.

He slowly, deliberately, receded into the bushes. All the while keeping his gaze fixed on her. And she on him. As he began to move behind them, passing through a particularly thick patch, she disappeared from view.

Gone just like that. From the window and from sight.

Definitely no ordinary bimbo. That complicated things, but now it was more of a challenge. He liked a challenge well enough. It honed everything. Even if the thrill only just surpassed the uncertainty he felt in his plan. It would make what he would do to her all the sweeter. And that was something he had not had before.

The Slasher disappeared further back into the foliage and began to move around the house.

Slowly.

Stealthily.

Intently.

He approached the back door and placed one gloved hand on the knob. The other slipped into his jacket pocket and grabbed hold of the lock pick inside. For a split second he thought, *There's no way it would be unlocked...right?* He couldn't resist not knowing and went to try it anyway.

Completely unlocked. He barely had to touch it. Either she was completely insane or she wanted him to come in that way.

Nice try, bitch, he thought. *But this ain't my first pig roast.* Still, it meant not needing to find another way in.

He pulled the hunting knife from its sheath and gripped it tight in his hand. Everything about this excited him. The anticipation. The pounding of his pulse. The only thing missing was the fear. She had ruined that for him. And for that, she would pay.

In he went. Still no sight of her. Shuffling into the den quickly before crouching behind the sofa nearest him. Scanning. Surveying. Watching for any sign of movement at all.

To his right, the brightly lit kitchen where he had first seen her. Polished pots hanging from above the center island. Countertops immaculate.

Just on the other side of the sofa the TV played, tuned to MTV where Robert Palmer was singing "Simply Irresistible." A halfeaten pizza sat on the table with a few Jolt cans strewn about.

There wasn't so much as a breath he could detect beyond his.

Think about it. Where could she be?

But all he could think about was what he was going to do to her when he caught her. *I'm going to slit her throat while I fuck her,* he thought. *God, yes!* That was the best. To feel them go limp and lifeless just as he finished.

Gingerly, he began up the stairs, careful to creep on the balls of his feet. Even in boots he could be quiet as a cat if done right. It had been a while since he'd skulked, but it was just like riding a bike. The muscles remembered.

At the first bedroom he thought, *Oh yes, here she is.* He could sense it. There, on the other side of the door. Couldn't explain how, it was just an instinct. The space on the other side felt fuller. In one forward motion he leaned into it with all his weight, meaning to knock her prone.

All he found on the other side of the door was an especially fluffy bathrobe in front of a Wham! poster.

He went from room to room, expecting to find her in each one. Instead there was nothing but unmade beds, empty bathrooms with no one lurking behind the shower curtain, no open windows or furniture disturbed, no sign or clue that she was or had been anywhere.

That left just one place left—the basement.

Good, he thought as one corner of his mouth twitched to a smile beneath his mask. When they run upstairs, there's a chance of escape. When they go down below ground surrounded by concrete, they don't have a prayer.

Back down the stairs he went, just as gingerly as he had gone up them.

Something hit him square in the chest from his left, connecting with his ribcage. Hard and wooden. What air he had in his lungs was forced out as he stumbled backward and landed hard on the floor. His chest screamed in pain. Every intake of air shredded at his insides.

She kicked his knife away and towered over him. Tall—taller than him at the moment, anyway—one hand on her hip, the other holding a Louisville slugger. The light from the kitchen travelled up the smooth skin of her legs, faded around her modest chest, terminating before it touched her face. He couldn't see her eyes, but from where he knew they were, the tiniest glints shone in them. Sharp lights of wrath boring down into him.

She put one foot on his chest and it sang bloody murder. Everywhere from coccyx to between his eyes cut into him in a way he had never known.

She knelt forward, foot still on his chest, showing her face fully to the light. Smiling.

The Slasher's eyes went wide as Ms. Six bent down and pulled off his mask.

Hair mussed from the mask and unkempt from years in

custody. Skin that had known the touch of coarse prison sheets and pillows more than sunlight and showed it. What started as a five o'clock shadow some evening long ago had grown into the dominant feature of his face. A snub nose desperately drew in one pained breath after another. His expression was the very picture of agony.

"I'm no doctor by any stretch, but if I had to guess, I'd say your sternum is broken."

He made to grab at her, every inch he moved a punishment. She swung down hard with the bat again and connected with the hand that lunged. Every bone in it destroyed.

He actually cried now. In pain. Pleading.

"And now your hand," she said, sucking air through her teeth. "Bummer, huh?"

She knelt down and began to pat him down. The lock pick, a pair of handcuffs, roll of duct tape, cloth pre-soaked in chloroform in a Ziploc bag, cellular phone, and a 3 Musketeers bar in case he got hungry later were all laid out on the floor next to him. Then she went for the cargo pocket in his pants. Her face changed from one of stern satisfaction to delightful surprise.

"Oh wow!" she said, taking out the note and reading it. "Is this my lucky day, or what?"

She went to the kitchen phone and eagerly dialed.

Fuck! The phone line.

"Hey, girl! It's Mandy. Guess who I've got hurt and helpless sprawled out in our main hall right now? ...The Sitter Slasher, that's who...I'm totally serious..."

He couldn't hear what the voice on the other end was saying, but it sounded excited.

"Caught him sneaking around *our* house. Can you believe it? I know! ...Right... Oh, I'll keep him alive, pinky promise. OK, see you soon."

She hung up and took a few short steps back over to him.

Mandy flipped him over and snapped the handcuffs around

each wrist. Tears streamed down his face as the unforgiving metal closed around his broken hand. With his face to the floor, he heard the sound of a door open. The Slasher felt himself being pulled forward by the collar of his jacket. Suddenly the floor gave way to a descending staircase….

Into the basement.

"Usually…"
She pulled him down one step with a *thud*.

"…we have to go looking…"
Then another.

"…for scum like you."

Gravity gave way and he went tumbling down the rest of the way, landing face down against a cold slab of concrete. The word "pain" lost all meaning as it took over and all but robbed him of his consciousness.

He could barely hear the sound of chains clinking from the pumping of blood in his ears, but he felt them alright. He knew that metal well. It was everywhere in prison. The bars, the windows, even the beds.

Steel slipped through his arms, cradling his back, and with one good tug he was lifted half a foot up.

A space appeared between his face and the basement floor.

The sound of chains being fed into something before a metallic grind pulled him the rest of the way up. He dangled there, suspended from the ceiling, turning in a languid circle.

The first thing he saw was a wall with all manner of tools affixed to a pegboard. Hammers, screwdrivers, drills, chainsaws, crowbars, hacksaws, hatchets, axes, even a flail. Mandy appeared in his view and placed the slugger in an empty space between two pairs of large hedge shears.

As he continued to spin—hearing the soft *clink* of her taking something else from the tool wall—something else came into view. Several display cases lining the wall perpendicular to the tools. In one was a leather cowboy hat, duster, and lasso with a plaque beneath that said: Denver Dodd, the Cincinnati Strangler. The next was a clown costume complete with a tuft of a green wig and comically large meat cleaver that said: Chuckles the Killer Klown. The next one housed a poncho fashioned out of garbage bags with a pigeon mask and a bloodied Venus de Milo just the right size to use as a club that said: Pigeon Man. The next one over was for Tapeface, then The Snuffer, and so on and so on.

He spun some more and saw a mirrored wall the length of the basement. Etched into it were the three Greek characters he saw at the entrance of the house, only here they were accompanied by the words Delta Kappa Theta.

Delta Kappa Theta. He had heard the name before. Spoken in the joint, always in hushed tones. An urban legend. The boogeyman's boogeyman, or in this case boogeywomen. Rumored to be a sorority who hunted killers, madmen, and psychos.

"But tonight, you came to our particular tuffet all on your own, didn't you, Mister Spider. Tonight," Mandy appeared before him, smiling and pretty and gripping an ice pick. She leveled it with his eyes. "You came to the *wrong* house."

The last thing the Sitter Slasher saw was his long-lost red. Only it was his own. And babysitters everywhere breathed a sigh of relief.

I never had much of a desire to write a slasher story. I like slasher movies, can't say I've read many aside from Psycho, *which I thought was great. So when it came time to write one—doesn't that just seem to be an inevitability for horror writers everywhere at some point—I wanted to do something that would pay homage to the subgenre and subvert it at the same time. So I thought, what if the killer finds a victim that makes him really, really regret having ever having laid eyes on her? That gets the same thrill out of killing that he does, does it for a purpose, sees it as a calling, and is better at it than him? And thus the sorority of Delta Kappa Theta was born; letters chosen because phonetically they sound close to the word "decapitate." One day I may refrain from resorting to word play, but…*

Who am I kidding? No I wont.

SCHOOL SPIRIT

Everyone at Clenoa Valley High School knew about the third-floor boy's room. Back when it used to be a junior high school, a seventh grader named Ernie Derkin hung himself in there. After it happened, Mr. Pasternak—the science teacher at the time—said that he remembered seeing Ernie in the east wing hallway carrying a bright yellow length of cord or rope or something, but didn't think anything of it at the time. Why would he? Next time anyone saw him, he was found hanging from a ceiling pipe by an electrical cord. I should know... I'm the one who found him. Caretakers gotta put up with a lot of crap and clean up a lot of mess. Comes with the job. But that sure was one thing I never thought I'd have to worry about.

I came in on a Sunday, you see. Often did. No one knew and I sure didn't have to, but sometimes it's best to get a jump on certain things like putting in work orders, stock invoices and the like. Monday morning the shit show starts and doesn't stop. Everything from relocating file cabinets for teachers who want them moved from one side of the classroom to the other to mopping up barf on sloppy joe day. So it's good to get that kinda stuff done rather than stick around till all hours of the night.

As soon as I came into the caretaker's office I could smell something funny. Just figured it was something that had spoiled in the fridge. But this wasn't some old lasagna or Chinese takeout. No. This was something rotten. Something *wrong*.

I thought a bird or maybe a raccoon had got itself trapped in the vents, and thanks to the heat that weekend the stink had carried. I went up to the roof and didn't find anything, which meant I'd have to go classroom to classroom, anywhere that had a vent. I looked through every room in the school, the main office, teacher's lounge, the gym, locker rooms, everywhere. Until there was just one place left.

No one ever used it, see. It was way out of the way, there were often roof leaks, and kids usually went in there just to smoke or screw around or make out or whatever they did. Meaning they also trashed the place regularly. It was so covered in graffiti there was no sense getting it painted no more, and the school just stopped caring about it. Meaning I stopped caring about it. Let 'em have their hideout for all I care, if it keeps them from messing up the rest of the joint. Which of course it didn't, but I'm sure if that rock had been kicked over they'd scatter and spread like cockroaches. So the way I figured, it was the least of two evils.

Up to the third floor I went and the closer I got to that boys' room the worse the smell got. And there he was. Just hanging there. Head bent forward, hair covering his face. Not moving. Yellow electrical cord pinched tight around his neck. Feet dangling there with one sneaker fallen off below him. I even tried to say something. How stupid is that! I got out as much as "Hey! You OK…?" before it all got to me and I lost my lunch right there. I remember thinking, What were you doing here kid? Why did you come in here? Why? This ain't no place for you.

Naturally when something like that happens fingers start pointing. So you better believe they pointed my way when the sad state of the bathroom was seen by people who had it in mind to make a fuss over it all of a sudden. Wasn't my supervisor's fault for telling me straight up not to give a shit about it or the school board's for not maintaining the upkeep with regular inspections. Nope. It was mine for having not kept it up to snuff. Ain't that a bitch!

He was twelve years old. Twelve, for Christ's sake! No one knows why he did it—not for sure. Though I got a pretty good idea.

You see...I put him there.

I went back in there for the first time since it happened just to get a proper look at things. It needed all the regular attention, a good mop and a scrub for sure. Hell, even a blast with the firehose. But also the mirrors were cracked, two of the four toilets didn't flush, the lights flickered, and man did it need a paint job. I could tell that at some point the walls had been painted a light blue, but you sure wouldn't know thanks to the graffiti. It was everywhere. Walls, stalls, sinks, garbage can, you name it. And every shitty thing you could think of.

"I wanna fuck Mrs. Ramis" ... "Damien James is a fag" ... "For a good time call Principal Higgins 277-4653"..."Here I sit broken hearted, came to shit and only farted" (OK that one I liked). One said "I Matter" and someone had crossed it out and replaced it with "No You Don't."

Remember, these were junior high kids.

And dicks, dicks, dicks! What is it kids like so much about drawing dicks?

Personally I really don't see any difference between writing something nasty on a bathroom wall and writing it online. No face, no thought, no consequences. That's all the damn internet is —a digital bathroom wall. People don't change, they just find new ways of being jerks to each other.

But the one that got me was the one I found on the back of the bathroom door—"Derkin sucks his mom's tit and likes it." Then someone else had written "I Sure Would!" in pencil below it. I didn't know his mom so wasn't quite sure what that meant. Maybe she had big tits or it meant he was a mama's boy or maybe it meant nothing. Just something shitty someone decided to write one day.

And not just written either, carved into it so that it would still be there even if it was painted over. Didn't notice it before because I'd propped the door open last time. And of course I didn't notice well before because I kept out of there.

Right about then I thought I could hear the sound of an electrical cord pulled tight and dangling against metal. And for the briefest of moments I thought I saw a blur of yellow in the reflection of one of the mirrors behind me. I was outta there faster than a kid running up the basement stairs! Every time I think about it a sick cold hits me inside.

So you see, I may not have been the one to tie the noose, but I could have done something about it beforehand and didn't. For that I've always felt terrible and now this was the punishment. The mind tricks of a guilty conscience I guess.

You see, I went to that school myself. It's OK if you find that pathetic. Hell, even I do. But sure enough if you were to look at the photos lining the halls you'll find one for the ninth grade class of '99. Third row, right side, at the back because I was so tall. Last name on the list — Clark Mackenzie. Most everyone just calls me Mac. Voted most likely to mop the halls of the same school he went to. I won't get into the how and the why of it all. Doesn't matter. Except to say that life don't exactly turn out like you think it's gonna. I do what I do and that's all there is to it.

It's changed a lot since then. On the surface at least. But truth is it ain't changed in any way that matters. The kids, the teachers, the principals, the parents, all of them were idiots then and they still are today. I know how that must sound coming from a guy who scrubs toilets for a living and doesn't have more than a high school education. But it takes a special kind of stupid to miss things that are right in front of your face. And that's what happened with the Derkin kid. He was quiet, kept to himself mostly, didn't seem to have a whole lot of friends, in fact if I ever saw him talking to anyone it was usually a teacher. But he was a good kid. A good egg. So of course he got shit on by the bad eggs.

I know how that is. Been there, done that, bought the toe tag. You want me to say I never thought about ending it all too? Well I can't. Not then, and not even now if I'm being honest. They say it gets better. One day this will pass and things will be better. I don't know about that.

Way I see it, it's not enough just to get through life. Just get by, keep your head down, tow the line. You need a reason to get up in the morning. To work hard, pay your dues, go through all the shit. Otherwise, what's the point? But ending things and thinking about ending them are very different. Besides, they could be a whole lot worse, right?

People use the phrase "kids these days"...kids these days got no respect. Kids these days are getting worse and worse. Nah. They've always been the same and they don't change much. A few good, far too many bad, and the rest you couldn't tell apart if you tried. They grow up to be just regular everyday assholes like anybody else.

Anyway, a year later the school was re-organized, dropping the "junior" and adding high school kids. And every day of that year that I was in the building I kept that third-floor bathroom so clean you could eat spaghetti and meatballs off the tile and happily ask for seconds. If there was so much as a wad of gum on the floor, I scraped it off right away. Even paid out of my own pocket to replace that door when the school wouldn't. But no matter what, that smell never went away. No one complained, and truthfully I don't think anyone else even noticed, but it was there. I could tell. You don't miss something like that.

It helped that kids tended to avoid it now after hearing about what had happened. It became that weird house on the block that no one wanted to go near. They'd dare each other to go in now and then but other than that they didn't pay it no mind.

One Sunday just after Christmas I came in again and found the glass of the trophy cabinet smashed. Most everything was still there except for one—the Clenoa Bucks basketball team's state championship trophy which they had just won the year prior. In its place, a turd. A ripe, rank dog turd fresh off the lawn. There, planted in the center was a small flag with "BUCKS SUCK!" written on it. There was only one possible culprit for something like this…Stonehill. The Stonehill Colts were the Bucks' bitter rivals since before even my time.

Shoulda called the police right then and there. But you know what? I wanted to catch them. Red-handed. Myself. These little bastards…day in and day out, leaving their garbage everywhere, writing "Your a bitch Mrs. Mueller" on their desks, plugging the toilets up with paper towels before they take a shit in them. But worst of all these particular little bastards didn't even go here.

Not on my watch. Not in *my* school!

I was going to leave them hogtied, pissing their pants and beggin' for mama until tomorrow morning. That'd show 'em.

So I got me a bat from the equipment room and set out looking for them.

It was a bad plan, I get that now. I didn't know how many of them there were and even if I did, unless I happened to take them all out faster than Bruce Lee, they'd be able to say I was the one that did it. But at the time I wasn't thinking clearly and didn't care.

They hadn't just smashed the trophy case. They'd busted lights, spray-painted tags —and more dicks of course—on the lockers, ripped up the seats outside the office, and knocked class pictures off the wall. These fuckers had it coming and I was gonna make sure they got it!

Once I got to the east wing I could hear them, the sound of

laughing and hollering traveling down the far stairwell. The one that led to—you guessed it—the third-floor boys' room.

I heard three different voices. And then a fourth. As well as the sound of spray cans. I can still remember gripping that bat so tight my knuckles hurt as I slowly and carefully cracked the door open just enough to get a peek inside.

I could see three of them dressed in dark hoodies indulging in one act of vandalism or another. Then suddenly another passed in front of the door. My heart nearly stopped beating. And there he was.

Dangling from the ceiling just like I found him. One shoe still missing. With no sound at all, he drifted down from the ceiling until his feet touched the floor. Then, just then, the lights that had been fine since everything else was fixed up began to flicker again.

He staggered jerkily toward one of the boys, who had his back to him. The yellow electrical cord slipped from around Ernie's neck, pulled tight between both fists before he threw it around the neck in front of him.

I let the door close and listened on the other side of it in horror as all Hell broke loose. There came pounding and hollering. The sound of bodies being thrown into stalls. The sick wet slap of heads hitting cement. Porcelain breaking as they hit the sinks.

The door was hurled open. I screamed and stumbled away as the scared face of the last boy appeared as he fled for his life.

Ernie Derkin caught him by the throat with his cord and pulled him back in. I'll never forget his face. Just as detached and dead as it was when I found him. No emotion. No life.

The door stayed open just long enough to see the boy's feet leave the ground, followed by the shattering of glass as he was hurled into one of the mirrors, cutting off his screams. Then all went quiet.

I just stayed there slumped down against the opposite wall, gripping the bat until finally my courage returned.

When I looked inside again there was a whole new kind of mess. Broken glass, metal bent out of shape, pools of blood leaking out beneath each body, and I can remember thinking that now it definitely would need a new paint job. The last thing I saw was Ernie, returned to his spot hanging from the ceiling like the first time I'd found him. Then in one slow motion he lifted a single finger to his lips and went:

Shhhhhhh…

So I went home—making real sure that no one saw me—fixed a bite to eat, drank a few dozen beers and wept. That's the truth of it. I wanted to see those boys pay for what they did, no lie there. But seeing them die was a whole different thing. It brought me no joy. But it would also be a lie to say that I was sorry it happened.

When you got it coming, you got it coming. Those four boys would grow up to be four men who would wind up doing even worse things. Hurting people. And getting away with it, you can bet on that.

Then of course there was Ernie. I guess since he checked out in there, he never really left. Either way, I can tell you for damn sure that I didn't sleep a wink that night.

My alarm went off at 5:00 AM just like every other day. I returned like I'd never set foot in the building since Friday and made the call. Police thought, as best as they could tell, that the four boys had got in a fight and killed each other. And I remember being scared, really scared, that I would be caught. That they would somehow pin this on me like they did Ernie's death.

But they didn't.

They questioned me of course, since I had access to the school and was the one who found the bodies. All I had to do was lie.

Had I been there at all since Friday?

No, sir.

Had I seen anyone or noticed anything out of the ordinary before I left?

No, sir.

Had I seen anyone or noticed anything out of the ordinary when I found them?

No, sir. Can't say I had, sir.

There was of course the weird detail about neck wounds from what appeared to be rope or wire of some kind when none was found at the scene, but with nothing to tie me to it, they moved on.

And that was it. End of story.

I don't know why I'm recounting this all now. Guess I just thought that before the years take me I'd better let someone know what really happened that day. So to whoever finds this after I die, now you know.

Until then, when it comes to the boy haunting the third-floor boy's room of Clenoa Valley High, it seems we have an understanding. I keep it clean, he keeps it safe.

But I swear, every now and then when I go in there I can hear the sound of an electrical cord pulled tight, grinding against the pipe. Catch odd blurs of yellow in the corner of my eye, dangling near the ceiling. And the soft whisper of a voice telling me *Shhhhhhh.*

Shhhhhhh...this is our little secret.

Though I can't help but wonder...was that meant to be an agreement...or a warning?

Shhhhhhh...

Or you'll be next.

I wrote this one over the course of a weekend; the fastest I've ever written a story other than Stay With Me. *A fact which, to me, meant that it must have been waiting to come out. I'll let you decide why.*

YOURS TRULY

New York Times — April 17, 1991

HIGHWAY HACKER APPREHENDED

A nationwide manhunt for the elusive Highway Hacker has finally come to an end. Curtis Weems, 38, of Flint, MI has been charged in connection with the string of disappearances and deaths reported throughout the country's interstate highways.

Reports of missing hitchhikers and people traveling alone have persisted across America for the past fourteen months, following the discovery of the remains of Renee Costas, a New Jersey woman missing and previously presumed dead along I-43 outside of Milwaukee. The FBI has conducted an extensive search for the killer dubbed the Highway Hacker due to the grisly state in which the victims were found. Five deaths have been linked to Weems, who was pulled over near Lansing, leading to a high-speed chase which ended in his arrest in rural Michigan. When officers on the scene looked in the trunk of Weems's 1977 Chevy Camaro, they found…

(Continued on page 4)

Letter #1 - May 5th, 1991

Special Agent Glen Lambert
C/O Federal Bureau of Investigation
935 Pennsylvania Avenue NW
Washington, DC
20535

Dear Agent Lambert,

First, my congratulations on finally catching me. You must really tell me how you did that sometime.

Second, your ingenuity notwithstanding the fact of the matter is that you've delayed my plans. Just a delay, nothing more of course. But certainly an annoyance. A stone in my boot. A pit stop, at best.

These accommodations are crude and I much prefer my coveralls to a jumpsuit but these are nothing when considering the work you and the so-called Department of Justice have taken me from.

But I'm sure you would understand if I just sat you down and explained it. I'm sure you would see reason. Therefore I invite you to Terre Haute State Penitentiary. Maybe I can even arrange for a couple of cold ones. What do you say?

Regards,
Curtis Weems

Letter #2 - June 14, 1991

Dear Agent Lambert,

Since I did not receive a reply in the affirmative — or any for that matter — to my last letter, can I safely conclude that you will not be accepting my invitation? I'd be remiss if I didn't point out that this could be an excellent opportunity career-wise. One-of-a-kind, even. Imagine the papers. The headlines. The prestige!
Just think about it.

Kindest Personal Regards,
Curtis Weems

The Daily News Journal — June 10, 1991

INSIDE HACKER'S CHOP SHOP

Interview with FBI Agent Glen Lambert
Conducted by Maxine Cromwell

CROMWELL: With me today is Special Agent Glen Lambert of the Federal Bureau of Investigation for this exclusive interview. Thanks for being with us, Agent Lambert.

LAMBERT: Thanks for having me.

CROMWELL: So let's get right to it, shall we? You have recently conducted a thorough investigation.

LAMBERT: Ongoing investigation.

CROMWELL: An ongoing investigation of the Highway Hacker's lair, known as the "Chop Shop." What can you tell us about that?

LAMBERT: First of all the FBI doesn't condone the name "Chop Shop" for an active crime scene. However...I've been investigating serial murders and crimes like these for seventeen years and I've never seen anything like it.

CROMWELL: How would you describe it?

LAMBERT: Carnage. That's the only way to describe it. People chopped, gutted and used for spare parts.

CROMWELL: My god.

LAMBERT: Yeah.

CROMWELL: Why would someone do this?

LAMBERT: It would take someone very sick and disturbed to do something like this.

CROMWELL: Is it true that the skin of the victims was used to upholster the interior of the Hacker's car, a nineteen seventy-seven Chevrolet Camaro? Nicknamed, "Sherrie."

LAMBERT: No comment.

CROMWELL: Is it true that figures or statues of some kind were made from a combination of cadavers, body parts, and automotive parts?

LAMBERT: No comment.

CROMWELL: Estimates for the total number of victims puts it in the thirty to thirty-five range. But there's been speculation that it could be as high as fifty. Perhaps even more.

LAMBERT: And that's all that is at this point, speculation. However, a proper count and identification effort for the victims is currently underway.

CROMWELL: You say the victims were used. Used for what?

LAMBERT: [inaudible]

CROMWELL: Are you alright, Agent Lambert? Do you need a minute?

LAMBERT: This interview is over.

Letter #3 - July 11, 1991

Dear Agent Lambert,

Clearly you are ignoring my correspondence. That is most disappointing. But I believe I know why that is…
You're afraid. Of what I've become. I who guzzles one ghost after another like nitro, siphoning them into my lady, my Sherrie, to ride haunted highways between this world and the next. If you only knew where the roads can lead, if you just know where to look and how. And have the balls to go there. All it takes is a little blood and the right set of wheels.
And the right fuel of course.
It was so easy, too. All I had to do was keep my head down, offer a few timid words—"yes, sir," "no, sir," "thank you, ma'am," "very kind of you m-m-miss"—act the part of a pitiful simpleton, and they bought it. Hook, line, and sinker. Every one of them.
Even your fiancée.
Oh, I'm sorry. Was that cruel of me? Was I the one who was

caught with another woman? And with your partner—Agent Martinez, is it?—no less. Oh yes, she told me ALL about it. The bruise on her eye said the rest. Honestly, Agent Lambert. That is no way to treat a lady. On second thought, maybe you should be thanking me. Think of the scandal had I not stopped to help her change that flat at just the right time that night. It was just one of life's little alignments.

Or perhaps it was fate that with your love forsaken mine was given what she needed to live. To ride.

And we will ride again!

Regards,
Curtis Weems

P.S. Still don't feel like talking?

National Enquirer — June 18, 1991

HACK AND SLASH HACKER'S STASH
By Tammy Starr

Today you're in for a treat, readers. I have the scoop on the Highway Hacker investigation. An inside source has provided some one-of-a-kind and prize-worthy information. The FBI crime lab has begun vivisecting the many weird and twisted things discovered in the Chop Shop. And let me tell you, it's juicy! In every way. Here's the list:

- (1) "Sally" 1959 Dodge Rambler + remains of Sally Gilmore Rutherford, OH.

- (1) "Marissa" 1961 Pontiac Tempest + remains of Marissa Di Giacomo. Brooklyn, NY.

- (1) "Sherrie" 1977 Chevrolet Camaro + remains of multiple

victims: upholstery leathered in human epidermis, stuffed with lower intestines, steering wheel fashioned from ribs, gear shift from sternum, gas pedal from phalanges, metatarsals, and tarsals, oil tank filled with human blood, one pair of lacquered eyeballs hanging from rearview mirror.

- (1) "Christy" 1981 Ferrari 308 GTS + remains of Christy Sanders. Berkeley, CA.

- (1) "Kitt" 1982 Pontiac Trans Am + remains of Katherine Dolianger. Paducah, KY.

- (2) Frigidaire Chest Freezer - 15 cu. ft. white: filled with various body parts.

At least twenty different victims have been identified from the remains. Aided by the license plates each bearing the names with black felt marker on duct tape. Among them, Diane Frasier, the now late fiancée of Special Agent Glen Lambert, who was reported missing months earlier. The only conclusion being that the rest of the victims were harvested and used in the bodywork of one car, while the others were...

(Continued on page 6)

Letter #4 - Undated (found following incident of July 19, 1991)

You cretin. You abslute fuckin monster!!! Have yo any idea what youve done? You KILLED HER! My love. My Sherrie...

Our babies!!!

Medical. Report - USP Terre Haute July 19, 1991
Attending physician: Dr. John Warren
Patient: Weems, Curtis Randall; Inmate #49510-042

Age: <u>38</u>
Sex: <u>Male</u>
Race: <u>Caucasian</u>
DOB: <u>7/18/1953</u>
Height: <u>6' 1"</u>
Weight: <u>280 lbs.</u>
Hair: <u>Brown</u>
Eyes: <u>Hazel</u>
Injuries: <u>Severe ballistic trauma of the cranium and brain tissue, hemorrhaging. Injuries sustained during altercation with prison guards, one of whom died in the process (see attached report).</u>
Treatment administered: <u>Intracerebral bullet removal via endoscopic trans-nasal craniotomy. Sutures applied. Blood transfusion [Type B+] 2-3 weeks recovery.</u>

Letter #5 - July 29, 1991

Ik now this might sound odd coming from me Agent Lambert. But I have to tell you somethng

Something has happened to me. I'm not quite sure how to explain this but ... I've changed. I can't quite say how or why but its true.

I used to be able to hear them. The voices of those I killed. I could hear Sherrie and our girls. All thier voices. Now I cant.

And somehow thats worse. I used to feel a sense of...god I hate to say it but comfort about all this. Purpose. Bliss. When I revived Sherrie with their parts revved the engine felt the wind on my face as I drove down the endless stretch of highways I was with her again. Listening to our song. But ever since the incident I can't see her anymore. Can't even hear her. She's just...gone.

She can't be gone.

But of course she is.

She looked at me like no one ever had.

We used to go to the drive-in. Out on Route 23 just the two of us. You know the first movie we went to see? The Shining. You would probably think I loved it an she hated it right? But nope. Other way around. I went an saw that flick three times becuase she loved it so. Which made me love it. In fact we were at the drive-in that night. All because of one stupid motherfucker who'd had one too many Budweisers and far too few bullets in the head. Turned out to be some snot-nosed punk kid of a congressman or some shit.

I was in the hospital for six weeks. While Sherrie was in the morgue.

How can this be? This just can't be.

Now there's a constant horrible pain in the pit of my stomach. If this is guilt, I sure don't want it. Caring is terrible.

Letter #6 - Aug 2, 1991

Dear Agent Lambert,

Well I found out a little bit more. Turns out the blood transfusion I got was from a nun visiting from St. Jude's. Sister Sophia. I've asked if I can see her. Just waiting for a answer back from the warden. I am entitled to spiritual and relgious counsel after all so I'm hoping the answer will be yes.

Hopefully she'll have some answers for me.

When I stop to think about all the things I've done. All the people I've hurt. Killed! I killed a guard. I've opened up someone's skull with a tire iron. I've chopped them up. Bled them. Used their skin for Sherrie's seats. How could I have done that??

Oh god...I can remember it all!

And for reasons I now realize are crazy. Completely crazy. Sherrie's not livin in the car. She's dead.

She's dead.

But I believed otherwise. Knew it. Saw it! In my head.

And the things I did because of it. I peeled off people's skin ~~Oh g~~

You wouldn't have any way to know this but I was just sick to my stomach.

Won't you answer me? Ever?

I wanted to tell you all this in person, but it seems I'm left with no other choice.

Your fiancée was nothing personal. You may think otherwise and I could understand why. Just wrong place at the wrong time. She felt no pain, if that's of any comfort to you. Such things are unthinkable to me. The lives I took were a necessity not a pleasure.

I assure you I didn't know who she was when I picked her up. How could I?

Like it or not we're all the other has anymore.

Curt

Letter #7 - Aug 5, 1991

Dear Agent Lambert,

I saw Sister Sophia today. She looked at me like no one ever does. The way Sherrie used to. But it wasn't her. She wasn't quite so old as I had imagined. Late 40s maybe. Kind eyes. When she smiled I swore I saw her again. If only for second. I asked her why she did what she did. And do you know what she told me?

Hebrews 9:22

She didn't recite it out for me. That's what she said. "Hebrews 9:22". And that's all she said. She kissed me on the forehead, crossed herself, muttered a prayer in Latin and left. I tried to get more out of her but the guards shut me down the minute I got excited.

When I got back to my cell. I looked up the passage she mentioned. Having been given a Bible when I entered this barred Hell.

"Under the law everything is purified with blood, and without the shedding of blood there is no forgiveness of sins."

That's Hebrews 9:22. I know what I have to do now. I have to atone. She gave me her blood so it could be spilled. I't ok. I'm fine with this. I hope my deth will bring comfort to the victims families and to you and when this is done I hope I see her again. My Sherrie. Maybe.

Yours Truly,
Curt

P.S. Nver thout a pnsil in the throat would make such a mess please excuse the blood stains...

GUARD POST LOG TRANSCRIPTION - TERRE HAUTE STATE PENITENTIARY — Aug 5, 1991. 9:08 - 9:12 PM. (Officers: T. Jones and F. Garvey on watch)

JONES: Post Four to Post Two.
GARVEY: This is Two.
JONES: You're not going to believe this but, incoming bogey.
GARVEY: What do you mean bogey?
JONES: Looks like a car coming up the service road. Due west.
GARVEY: I see it. Intercepting.

ACTS OF VIOLENCE

[2 minutes, 41 seconds of silence follow]

JONES: Post Four to Post Two, come in.
GARVEY: Yeah this is Two. Bogey's gone now.
JONES: It just left?
GARVEY: Yep.
JONES: Did you get a make?
JONES: Nah, too dark. A Dodge? Maybe a Chevy?
JONES: Was that music I heard?
GARVEY: Yeah. "Oh Sherrie" by Journey.
JONES: Steve Perry.
GARVEY: Huh?
JONES: "Oh Sherrie" was by Steve Perry.
GARVEY: Whatever. Post Two, over and out.

—END OF TRANSCRIPT—

Letter #8 - September 6, 1991

Attn: Seymour Blatch, Director

    I tender my resignation effective immediately. Please cease all correspondence and have returned to sender. Thank you.

Best,
Glen Lambert

This story started as a variation on an urban legend. The way it goes is that a good, upstanding individual who would never harm anyone is involved in an accident or near death experience of some kind leading to them needing a blood transfusion. It then turns out that the blood came from a maniac or serial killer—because of course it did—and how it ends varies from one telling to the next. I just flipped things around. And while it may seem heavily influenced, some might even say cribbed, from Stephen King's Christine, *I actually had not read the book when I wrote it. I had seen the film though; some of John Carpenter's best work, I think. So one way or the other it was surely an influence, but not as much as you might think.*

EVERY HUNT IS A COLD ONE

WHITE.

Endless, blinding white as far as the eye could see. Hope was sick of it. No, sick wasn't right. Sick didn't even begin to do justice to the hatred she had for it. And the feeling was mutual.

Darkness was easy. It could be honed, hidden in, used to her advantage. All she had to do was stay still and silent, and it would welcome her like an old friend. But up here everything was exposed. Each breath showed in plumes of ghostly mist. Every step crunched in the snow, telling anyone and anything within earshot where she was. Up here there was nowhere to hide.

And it was cold. Nothing new, of course. It was always cold now, everywhere. She could barely even remember a time before the Freeze. So long ago it seemed more like a story Daddy had read her. Most of what she knew had come from him. But somewhere deep in the frozen recesses of her memory, she recalled something other than white, and black, and the occasional red of blood. A time when winter was just one of the seasons. Of greens and blues. Sun and water. Other things she took for granted like wheat fields and pavement. They were still there of course. Just buried under tons of snow.

She couldn't think about that now. If she started, she'd never stop.

And the hunt was on.

The tracks led east, toward the City. She knew it was called Calgary, or had been once, but to her it, was just "the City". Daddy said never to go to the City, but today she didn't have a choice. She and Adam hadn't eaten in days, and even if she caught something, the meat couldn't always be trusted. And even if it could, it would barely be enough to go around.

Everything was running out. Food, water, wood. Time. They had gas up until a short while ago, enough to light the lamps at least. Now everything was scarce. Most of it for good, like ammo. There would never be more of that unless she was lucky enough to find some. Every tree nearby was either cut down, frozen solid, or buried under snow long ago, so most of the time having a fire was impossible. Only if she decided to burn that which she needed to survive or could not bear to see go up in flames. Oh, what she would give to feel one right now. Water wasn't a problem, but even in the shelter, it couldn't always be melted enough to drink.

Everything ached. She hadn't eaten in days and her bones showed through her skin. And Adam, he didn't look well. Weak and feverish when last she saw him. That was two days ago. She could hardly bear being away for so long but had been needing to venture further and further from home to catch anything at all for a while now.

This world was something no boy of six should have to face. He was her only saving grace, but sometimes she was sorry for bringing him into it. He had never even left the shelter.

Wind howled against her, biting through every crease and crack it could find. Though she was covered from head to toe, bound up in thick white layers like a mummy, it still got through. It always got through. The tracks were at risk of disappearing before her, but fortunately they were deep enough to last for a bit at least. Her own steps left very little trace thanks to a trusty pair of snowshoes fashioned out of a pair of tennis rackets. Daddy said they were used in a game "pencil neck candy asses" used to play.

An hour passed.

Then two, during which she lost feeling from the waist down. Not completely, just enough to feel frostbite setting in.

Well into the third hour she found herself at the City limits. It appeared all of a sudden out of the blowing snow, looming before her like a ghost. The deer had gone right into it, its hoof prints now round and hard. Fresh.

As she crossed a bridge over the river, Hope took the bow from around her torso and fit it with an arrow. Her hand briefly fell to her side, patting the ice pick that dangled there clipped to her belt, telling her *I'm here if you need me*.

Signs, street lamps, traffic lights, whole buildings, all encrusted with snow and ice. She kept her head low, just beneath the drifts lining each side of the street. They had been cars once. Now little more than dead machines. Useless as the corpses inside them. There were a number of things to watch for, and her prey was just one of them.

Amazing to think any animals could have survived in this at all, let alone for so long.

As she followed the deer tracks, she spied another set. Long and flat. A rabbit. Not a very big one and they went in the other direction, but something to eat was not to be passed up.

They grew fresher and fresher as she followed them down a side street. This, added with the wind easing up for the first time in days, reduced to a frigid breeze, made her job far easier.

And then she spotted it. So still it was nearly invisible, had it not been for that single wide leporine eye looking her way from the side beneath long ears. Wondering if she saw. It just sat there twitching its distinctly non-bloodied nose. Didn't appear to be sick.

Slowly, she raised the bow. Not enough to aim yet, just enough to size things up. To declare the intent to herself.

The rabbit crouched, making itself small.

She stopped moving. If it ran she would have to be quick.

It remained still.

Her muscles flexed just enough to move the bow up again, while her other hand, or at least two fingers of it, began tensing the arrow against the bowstring.

A massive white paw swiped out at the rabbit from between two drifts. It ran away in a flash while Hope froze, inside and out.

Out stepped a mountain of a monster. The biggest bear Hope had ever seen in her life. There hadn't been many times, and they had all been from afar. And always with Daddy there, ready with his shotgun. He said that before the Freeze they used to live way further up North. How something so big made so little sound was a mystery. Despite its size, the bear was sickly. Thin. Weak and hungry. Its bones showed through the patchy white fur that was pink in some places from having fallen out. Huffing out one hard, labored breath after another through jagged teeth. The skin around one eye hung loose in the socket, and the eyeball along with it. And there, wetting the nose, was the telltale sign of the Cold—blood. Its snout was dripping with it. Probably from eating too many that had caught it.

The bear turned and looked right at her.

Its growl sounded desperate and weak, but still enough to send her running without a second thought. Hunter had become prey.

Nothing but the sound of massive footfalls, punishing the snow beneath it with every step, followed by the forced huff of each hungry breath.

Hitting it with an arrow—*if* she hit it—wouldn't even slow it down, only piss it off. Outrunning it became less and less of a possibility with every inch it gained on her.

But size wasn't everything.

She took a hard left down an alley, between two buildings. Skidding across the snow, digging a deep scar into it. The bear was fast. Heavy. Determined. Luckily, though, the bear couldn't pivot worth a damn, coming almost to a complete stop in order to follow.

She got a good thirty feet ahead, but the alley was long and solid with nowhere to turn. When it charged after her again, it meant it. She felt the impact of its weight in the frozen ground.

This may have been a bad idea.

The end was in sight, the narrow white around her ready to open back up into a blinding one the nearer she got to it.

A blast of hot breath hit her. The first warm thing she had felt in days. At least it would be the last thing she would remember.

A gunshot.

She hadn't heard one for years and stopped in her tracks. So loud even the bear halted.

Another tore through the air, pinging off the wall behind her. She hit the deck and the bear continued forward, trying to squeeze out of the narrow alley.

Then came a third shot. The bear hit the ground. The last of the air escaping its lungs—a prelude to the unnerving, unyielding silence that followed.

Hope knew all kinds of silences. There was the silence of the City, lacking not only sound, but life. The gentle one that falls over the entire world when it snows on Christmas morning. The harsh one which tethers the absence of affection between two people. The type that passed between her and Adam when they had nothing to talk about, which was often. Or just a lack of sound, pure and simple. But this was no common silence.

A frigid breeze blew through the City, bringing with it a different kind of chill altogether, overtaking the one she felt in her body. Nowhere near so hard as before, diminished to a nosy whisper. Her perforated breath, forced out between chattering teeth as she shifted gears down from full throttle to idle, hacked and stalled until it finally produced a sound.

"H-hello?"

No response. Just the wind biting through every thin fold of her clothing, telling her to leave. This was a silence she had never known before. Deliberate. Irksome. The guilty quiet of someone who was there but chose not to speak.

She lifted one foot to start moving away.

Another shot rang out. Instantaneously, the ground where her step would have fallen exploded in a pop of snow.

For a second—just a *second*—she had caught a flash coming from somewhere in the murky white distance. The message was clear.

Don't move!

Her heart raced and pumped ice water through her veins.

Then she heard something.

Crunch...crunch...crunch...crunch...

Hushed. Almost languid. Each *crunch* grew just a little louder. Closer.

She ditched the makeshift snowshoes and made a dash for it, the crunch of her own footsteps interrupting those that approached until she couldn't hear them. Any second she expected them to be ceased by a final shot, the world of white replaced by one of darkness forever.

The cover of what had once been an underground parkade came into view on the other side of the road. Nearly swallowed by drift after drift, but accessible. She ducked between snow-covered cars and slid smoothly down a hill.

Another shot. It missed, hitting the ground right next to her.

She didn't stop to look back as she made for cover. Couldn't afford to. From somewhere behind came the series of metal clicks of a reload.

Almost there. So near that the shadows touched her covered face now.

The next shot she felt as well as heard, screaming its ugly red pain into her foot just below the ankle, falling to one knee as she reached the shelter of darkness.

No time for pain, she thought, ducking behind a concrete pillar for cover.

Crunch…crunch…crunch…crunch…

She didn't even have time to appreciate being out of the endless wind and snow for the first time since leaving home, howling away just on the other side of the pillar like the churn of a violent sea.

Her hand fell to the ice pick again. It wasn't there.

Hope fit the bow with another arrow, having lost the first one somewhere during the chase.

Anything center mass is going to be protected by thick layers of padding. No good.

Same with the legs, and a wound there wouldn't prevent him from firing.

A headshot would do it, but easier said than done.

Crunch…crunch…crunch…crunch…

With a long sharp breath, Hope steadied herself and made a move.

The shot came right away. She didn't even have time to aim, let alone fire…but then she hadn't meant to. Let him waste his shot. And then came the sound she was waiting for, the metallic clicks of a reload.

Everything moved in slow motion. She took aim, getting her first real view of the hunter. About thirty yards away. Red coat.

Face covered by a ski mask and goggles. Holding a rifle which was half a second away from becoming dangerous again.

She fired. It missed completely, carried off by the wind and disappearing into the white. She took shelter behind the pillar and drew another arrow.

Four left.

The next shot hit the other side of the pillar.

Gotta make the next one count.

Crunch…crunch…crunch…crunch…

Much faster this time.

She bolted from behind the pillar, leaving a trail of bloody footsteps behind her. Stumbled and fell onto her back while trying to shoot the arrow at him as he rushed her.

All this for a rabbit, she thought as the butt of the rifle came down hard right in the middle of her forehead, robbing her of what little light there was as darkness took over.

For the briefest of moments, she was thankful.

Daddy was strict but nice. He taught her how to plough and sow the field. He taught her how to fish. How to drive the tractor. How to shoot, how to hunt, how to dress and clean a kill.

Daddy made her read scripture. Every day. No excuses. When she was finished, she'd start again. Daddy said the world was going all to Hell thanks to the rosary-rattlers, the heathen liberals, the Jews, the Muslims, and the queers. Well, he was right about things going to Hell at least. Only this Hell had frozen over. They didn't have a TV, but Daddy kept a radio for emergencies. The voices said that the ice caps had melted and released diseases trapped for millions of years.

Then one day, the radio voices stopped. Then there was only one country. One land. Its flag was white, but it didn't surrender.

Daddy said, "We done fucked this world up so bad it's fuckin' us back." He said that the End Times had come with ice rather than fire. That reminded her of a poem by Robert Frost that she had read in the school library:

> Some say the world will end in fire,
> Some say in ice.
> From what I've tasted of desire
> I hold with those who favor fire.
> But if it had to perish twice,
> I think I know enough of hate
> To say that for destruction ice
> Is also great
> And would suffice.

Daddy made her do things. Not for himself, never for himself, but to replenish the earth. It said so right in the Book of Genesis when Lot had lain with his daughters. There was never any joy in it for him. He was just doing right by God. She wasn't sure she believed him, but she didn't hate him. Could never hate him. After all, he gave her Adam. And together, no matter how cold the world had become, they were a family.

Daddy went out hunting one day. Six years ago. And since then, he was gone.

When Hope woke, it was to the feel of something she hadn't known in so long that she had nearly forgotten it: warmth. The crackle of a fire came from behind her, heating the backs of her arms and neck. So nice, such a relief she could have cried. The wind was gone now, diminished from its constant howl to a distant whisper somewhere off to her right. Even more distant now that it was behind the soft guitar notes of a bossa nova tune trickling through the room. Refined and alien to her even before the Freeze.

Everything was numb. A sensation she had grown familiar with thanks to frequent subzero temperatures and frostbite. This was different though. Barely any feeling at all from the waist down, and she couldn't feel her left leg at all. Probably a good thing considering that was the foot that had been shot, but the rest would almost certainly be blistered and black this time. Might even lose a toe.

Her cheeks, the bridge of her nose, anywhere the wind could slip through burned. Oh, the tragic irony in the fact that cold could burn, reminding her of that poem again.

The fireplace cast a shadow play against the surfaces of everything in front of her, the dim orange glow now keeping the odious blue dark of night at bay. Her vision was blurry to a point of near invisibility, but she could just make out candles on a table. Others sat around it, not moving but looking her way.

Her head throbbed with a dull but persistent pain throughout her head. It would have been far worse had it not been for the drugs pumping through her bloodstream. She smelled clean, soap mixed with a vague but unmistakable antiseptic smell of iodine. Liquid water being a tough enough thing to get in the first place, she hadn't had the luxury of a bath in a long time.

For a moment she thought everything might be ok. She flexed her muscles, meaning to reach up and rub the haze from her eyes, only to find her arms strapped down to those of the chair she was in. A belt around her midsection held her tight to the back of it.

Footsteps approached. Same pace as before, the crunch of snow replaced by the jingling of keys.

"Ah, you're awake," came a slightly nasal voice just beyond the cloud of her vision. He placed something in the middle of the table—her nostrils were filled with the savory smell of cooked meat, garlic, and rosemary—came around the table past one of the other guests (who still hadn't moved or spoken since she regained consciousness) and knelt down next to her. Bearded and balding. A bit sickly as though his face had once been fuller. Nothing much to look at aside from his kind brown eyes. It all felt shallow though. Thin ice in April.

"What's your name?"

"Hope," she answered with little breath.

"Hope," he echoed, soothed by the very sound of it. "Perfect." His hands went to her face. Roughened and calloused from years of being forced to use them, but like his face, it was only on the surface. The palms still held some semblance of their former refinement. They had once been treated, cared for. Precise. Vapor trails streamed out from the candles as he guided her head upward, tickling her face from the slight tremor that shook his fingers. A thumb pulled down the bottom lid of one eye and then the other. "How are you feeling?"

"Dizzy," she said.

"Hmm, you will for a little while, but the anesthetic should be wearing off soon." He stood, rattling the keyring clipped to his belt, and went around to the other end of the table. "Well I hope you're hungry because we've got a proper feast tonight."

"Feast?" The word felt foreign on her lips.

"Oh yes. It's not every day we have a guest for dinner, is it, kids? But where are my manners? I'm Murray, and this is my family. Well…"

Her vision cleared up. Sitting on either side of a long dinner table sat two bodies—a boy about ten and a girl about eight. Dressed, groomed, a full set of cutlery set out before them. White plastic bags covered their heads, taped at the neck with blood smeared where the noses would be. Smiley faces were drawn on them in thick black felt marker.

"I guess it's our family now." The smile on his face was all too real. "Kids, say hello to Hope. Your new mother."

She tried to flex, test the strength of leather straps holding her in place, praying for any sign of weakness in them. This time her movement sent a tube connected to her hand swaying. It was connected to an IV suspended above her from a stainless steel stand next to her. She followed it down to the floor and saw that the chair she was in had wheels on it. Some of the feeling returned to her legs…to one of them at least.

"Oh god," she said, looking at the steaming dish on the table. "Where did that meat come from?" Hope nudged herself away from the table and looked beneath. She saw only one leg. With her entire body and soul, she screamed. In pain. In sorrow. In hopes that someone would hear and come to help. But there was no one.

"I understand that you're upset," said Murray, "but it needed to be amputated and…well…waste not." He cut himself off a piece with his fork and knife and began to chew. "Not bad, actually. Anyway, you won't need it here. I'll take good care of you. I promise."

Maybe he was right. Maybe this wasn't so bad. *I'm tired of hunting, tired of fighting, tired of the cold. But…*

"My boy…"

"What boy?"

"I have a son. He's out there, alone. Has been for days."

Murray stood from his seat. "Good god! Why didn't you say so?"

Must have slipped my mind, asshole.

"Did you hear that, kids? You're getting a new brother too. Where is he?"

"North…north-wes—" Her head fell forward and hung.

Chair legs squealed across the floor followed by the same hurried footsteps as before. Hands trembling, he lifted her head up, thinking she had fainted. As soon as she caught a glimpse of his face close to hers, she lunged.

Hope bit into the freshly shaved skin of his neck. He jerked away, but she held on for dear life with every tiny dagger in her mouth.

They collapsed to the floor, toppling the wheelchair and the IV pole. She fell on top of him, ripping and tearing back and forth until the jugular broke and the initial gush of blood became a torrent.

His hands flew to his neck as he tried to stop the leak, wailing as he climbed frantically to his feet. He rushed back to the other side of the table, grabbed a cloth napkin up, and pressed it against the wound.

"Why would you do that? Huh?! Why—" The cloth of the napkin had turned from white to red in no time. "Oh god."

He hurried down the hall and disappeared. Assuming Murray could stop the bleeding, Hope figured she had two minutes before he returned.

Hope spat what blood she had in her mouth onto the floor, careful not to swallow any. It was the first warm thing she had had in her mouth in a long time. She didn't even mind the taste. And she was so hungry.

No. Not now. You went this long without resorting to that. *Now is not the time.*

Still strapped to the wheelchair, she wriggled herself over to the blood she had spat, and tried to get as much of it as she could on her hands.

Not enough.

From the bathroom down the hall, all she heard was things slamming and his wailing in pain and fear for his life as it poured out of him.

She wriggled further to the trail of blood he'd left behind him, expecting any moment he might return, neck bandaged, towering over her, with something blunt and nasty to pound what was left of her to death.

Hand sufficiently wet now (thankful for the small blessing of not having to look at it), Hope twisted her wrist against the leather strap and freed herself of its grip. With one bond gone, the other was no problem, nor was the belt around her waist.

She grabbed a knife from the table and crawled on her elbows beneath it. Hunched and waiting for him to reappear.

"C'mon," she fumed. "C'mon, you fucker." Every second he didn't show, the more she felt it coming. "Come on!"

No more sound came from the bathroom. Eventually she realized that it was going to stay that way, and was lost to quiet sobs.

Can't I just lay here by the fire? she thought. *That's all I want. Warmth and heat. A world of lovely golden light and no more of the cold.* And lay there she did, allowing herself a few precious moments of this small pleasure. It stretched out into the longest, most unbearable sigh. Cruel really, because it could not last.

Hope crawled out from under the table, flipped the wheelchair back upright, and — after a few failed attempts — hoisted herself into it.

Carefully, slowly, she wheeled herself down the hall.

He could still be alive. She knew that. He could be crouched, quietly waiting for her to come to him. But she needed those keys. Without them, the journey back home would be impossible.

Not a sound from the other side of the door. Cautiously she pushed it open with the knife. A quick peek inside before ducking back around the doorjamb.

No movement. No breath.

She looked again and took in the few details she could see properly.

White and black tiles laid out in a checkered pattern on the floor. Walls painted in a smooth eggshell. Countertops of hard mottled marble. And a real porcelain clawfoot tub at the far end.

Everything in here bled, marred by smears and spatters of blood. It streaked over the rim of the bathtub where a single leg stuck out over the side. Dripped off a hand that stood up in the air, its fingers twitching.

Funny how this tiny show of movement confirmed his demise more than absolute stillness. Even so, she approached ready for anything, clutching the knife so hard it hurt.

There he lay, drenched and red and lifeless. Eyes still open, the expression on his face vacant. Looking for something he would never see. His other hand rested on his thigh, holding a surgical needle fit with stitching. Too little too late.

He couldn't harm her now. He was no longer the hunter. Just another dead thing. Still, there was an eerily tragic way about him. A man looking for company, driven mad by loneliness, despair, solitude, and loss. Ceased to be.

She thought about crawling into his arms while he was still warm. Just to feel it once more. An embrace. The feel of being in someone's arms again. Even an enemy. Even a corpse. To know it was real once again and always had been.

At least, that was how she saw him. It was a lot better than he deserved.

Hope unclipped the keys from his belt. He moved in her mind, but nowhere else as she wheeled herself out the door, leaving him truly and finally alone.

Back at the farm. Amazing she still saw it that way, even after all this time. It was little more than a frozen, broken-down husk of what had once been. The house was gone completely. Only the barn remained and it was badly in need of repair. But it would always be where she fed chickens. Where she played and swam. Learned how to plant. How to grow. How to shoot. How to survive.

Using the rifle as a crutch, she awkwardly got out of Murray's truck. Some silly part of her thought maybe, just maybe, the wind would relent just this once. But no. It bit into every haphazardly covered part of her all the same.

She made her way into the barn. The roof was full of holes that had fallen in with the weight of snow and ice, snowflakes swirling down from above, and the rest looked like it could go anytime now.

Thankfully not much snow had covered the trap door to the shelter since she left, and clearing it away would not have been easy standing on one leg. She gave the handle one unsteady tug and nearly lost her balance. The second time it was flung open.

"Adam?" she called. "Adam, come quick. Mama needs your help."

It was true. Not just to get into the shelter, but to get back to the penthouse, to get whatever food, provisions, and supplies they could from it. She had kept him safe and sound up to this point, but with everything she would need his help from now on. Far too much to ask of a boy of six, but now there was no choice.

No response from inside.

She began to hop down the stairs, bracing herself on her elbow along the railing. The rifle crutch missed the step it was supposed to land on and she fell. Only a few steps, but now every inch of her hurt.

On her side, she craned her neck upward and saw him sitting with his back to her not far away. Still covered by the blanket she had wrapped around him herself, staring at a wood burning stove of nothing but cold ashes.

"Adam," she choked out. Still no response.

Hope crawled over to a nearby chair covered with clothes and blankets she had found elsewhere and hobbled over to where he was.

At first she thought he might still be alive and tried to shake him awake. But there was no color left in his face. She couldn't even bear to say his name again.

Hope took him in her arms and wept. Her boy. Her son. All she had left, now also claimed by the cold. She rocked him back and forth, held tight against her breast. He was still warm…and she was so hungry.

So hungry.

This story came from a very weird place. It was during a time when everyone was stuck in their homes like a bunch of hermits, afraid of a virus that seemed to be everywhere, during a time of the year I loathe, with all manner of personal issues escalating from nuisance to calamity. And all on top of countless other ongoing real world horrors, and while publishing my first novel, and...and...and...you get the idea.

I always hope for the best, of course. And that was how I originally planned to end this bleak little tale. But experience has far too often told me a different story. One where hope can be as hard to find as grass in winter. Don't get me wrong, I don't mean to sound pessimistic or anything—well, maybe a little—all I'm saying is that there's a reason why, in addition to hoping for the best, we also plan for the worst.

That's where this story came from. That's how it started, continued, and ended.

With the worst.

MATTERS OF THE HEART

THEY SAY LOVE IS CRAZY. AND SO IT IS. I JUST NEVER knew how crazy until I was killed.

I don't remember everything about the day it happened. Just bits and pieces, really. I remember leaving third-period English but not my teacher's name or what they looked like. However, I do remember stopping in the girl's room on the way out of the school. Nothing extraordinary about that except for the fact that I remember looking in the mirror like anyone would have. No different than countless other times. And I, Amy Elizabeth Warner, was certainly no different from anyone else in that way.

Sixteen years old and twenty-nine days I was when it happened, my birthday having been just under a month earlier, in August. My gingerbread locks were held back with a hair band. A light dusting of freckles across my nose and cheeks. But it just so happened to be the last time I would see my own reflection. When you're dead, it's the little things you miss.

I remember walking home and that it was a nice day out. Fall, but just barely felt like it. Still warm, the trees made all the lovelier by a change in color. The best autumn had to offer. That isn't much but what memory of it I still have is vivid as ever. Like trying to recall how a postcard made you feel. Golden leaves with no warmth left to love. Just a flat background, cracked and hardened as an old painting that hasn't been cared for, which is beautiful and perfect but holds no depth.

I remember a car pulling up next to me, a brand new 1988 Corvette to be exact.

"Hey, good looking. Going my way?" It was Robbie. Him I remember perfectly. With that wavy hair of his the color of warm sand. A smile that made me ache in every possible way and dimples to match.

Then what did I say? Something stupid like, "I dunno, stud. Going somewhere fun?" Shut up. I was trying to be cute.

He said he knew just the spot, so I hopped in.

What can I say? I liked him. He was dreamy, had a cool car, and the way he looked at me...there were no words for it. What's a girl to do?

As we passed through town I remember seeing that stores had already started to bring out Halloween stuff. At first I thought we were headed for Pheasant Run, an area just North of town where people sometimes went hunting. But Robbie said it was just a little bit further, overlooking the lake.

I remember that the top was down on the car. There's just something about being swept up by the wind while driving that makes you feel free and like there isn't a care in the world. And then I remember opening my eyes—I think they were closed briefly while I surrendered to the moment—when I saw something in the passenger's side mirror. A moped coming our way. I couldn't see the one riding it but I thought immediately of Simon.

Simon Crease. We were friends in third grade when he lived next door to me. He had a pool, and I liked to swim. But from the day I showed up in a two-piece for the first time, things were different with him. He got clingy, you might even say obsessed. When he asked me to go to Spring Fling with him and I said no because I'd already said yes to Robbie—though that wasn't the whole truth—it was more hatred than heartache I saw in his eyes. I definitely remember that.

I remember then fearing that the moped was following us, but it took a turn and disappeared down the road.

We found a place to park and then I remember us going for a walk into the woods. Holding hands. He brought a blanket so we could lay down on the grass. It was a beautiful spot by the lake. Nothing but the noteless chorus of leaves rustling in the autumn breeze.

I remember him looking at me and I said, "What?"

He just shook his head and said, "Nothing."

When he looked at me I felt like I was the only one who mattered. Like we were the only two in the whole world. I met his eyes with mine.

I said, "My heart is yours," and leaned in to kiss him.

I remember hearing something behind us. The snap of a twig. I spun around and looked behind me. Nothing there but a scattering of shadows from the swaying trees that lingered a little too long for my liking, making it appear briefly that someone may be passing through the woods.

And then he said…I'll never forget this…

"Promise?"

I didn't even see the knife. But I sure felt it.

The last thing I remember seeing while still in my body was his face. It didn't change. Not one bit. He still looked at me with the same love and devotion as a moment ago. Maybe even more.

Then things went dark. My view shifted from looking up at his face to looking down at the back of his head. As soon as he moved I saw me. Or what was me. Now an empty shell. Covered with blood. Still shocked. The knife buried to the handle in my chest. My blood spilled out, soaking the blanket, the grass, even the soil.

He dragged me with the blanket to the edge of the woods,

then to a small shack, near indistinguishable from the trees surrounding it. Inside was little more than a mattress on a box spring, and an old oil lamp on a shelf above it. Just the one small window next to the bed, no other source of light. He took off all my clothes, and then his. He was hard enough to split diamond. He spread some of my blood across his palm, wet himself with it, and slid inside me.

He gasped.

I didn't feel a thing.

When he was done he grabbed hold of the knife, still in my chest, and pried me open. Surgically, tenderly, he cut out my heart. He stared at it like he did to me not long ago. Then he licked it.

The muscles convulsed, spurting the last drops of blood across his bare chest. He slid a jar of a clear, almost yellowish fluid from beneath the bed and placed my heart inside. He then placed the jar on the shelf next to the oil lamp and lay down on the bed with my body.

He said he loved me and stroked my hair.

I remember thinking, *Why did you do this?*

Then, as if he had heard me, he said, "Because I love you." He stared lovingly into my dead eyes. The flicker of the oil lamp in their reflection giving but the faintest imitation of life. "Think of all the things I saved you from—work, taxes, divorce, depression, addiction, pain, childbirth, growing old and sick and ugly. Now you can just be mine, and me yours. Forever."

The sick thing is, he was right. In his way.

Stranger still, I wasn't even that mad. Not at the time, at least. I should have been, right? The truth is, if I had to do it all again, I would. I don't think I could even say why except that he was my first.

And last.

My only.

I watched as he took me down to the lake, walked into it

holding me in his arms. Washed me. Dried me. Combed my hair and sewed me back up. He covered me with the bedsheets and bid me goodnight. Said he would see me tomorrow. Then he left.

The night passed and true to his word, he returned the next day around when he would have been done with school. And since the next day was a Friday, he said we could spend the weekend together. Just the two of us.

We talked for two days. Well, he talked. I listened.

He told me all about how when he brought home a bad report card his old man loved to give him a taste of his knuckles, belt, or boot. When he was younger he'd get the same for wetting the bed. His old man said it was for his own good. He told me about the animals he had hurt and the ways he had hurt them. He told me about how he used to watch his aunt undress, not because of her body, but what was inside, what things looked like beneath the skin.

He told me how good a listener I was, how pleased he was that I was his first. And you always remember your first. On that, we agreed.

To think that someone so handsome and charming could be what he was. But that's how nature works. Some of the most deadly things dazzle the eye and ensnare the senses. The colors that catch the eye are so often poisonous. That which draws our eye is so often a prelude to death.

He left late Sunday afternoon.

The next day he visited again, and this time he said that I had been reported missing. Flyers had already been posted and there was talk of organizing a search party. It wasn't long before a candlelight vigil was held and my parents appeared on TV begging anyone with knowledge of my whereabouts to come forward. If there was anything that caused me to hate him, it was that. The worry he brought to my family.

I watched my body become cold and stiff—which didn't seem to affect his stiffness at all—and though I had no way to tell, I imagine that my body had begun to smell. Decomposition was visible by this point. He either didn't seem to mind or didn't notice. Then the next day he came to visit, he told me that our time was up. Said we had grown apart and it was time to move on.

I remember him dragging his fingers along the smooth side of the glass jar as he stared at my heart and said, "I'll always have this."

He gathered me up in the bedsheets and took me to his car. We drove for what felt like not very long, but it was hard to tell. Time becomes weird after death. Eventually we came to another patch of the woods where he had a grave already dug. He put me in it, gently, and dumped one shovelful of dirt after another on top of me. He covered the freshly turned earth with a good deal of sticks and leaves to cover his tracks.

He stood, went to a nearby oak tree, and, with the knife he had used to cut out my heart, carved another into the bark, surrounding our initials.

RB + AW

No one had ever done anything like that for me before.

And then he just stood quietly for a while, looking at the spot where he had buried me.

"Goodbye, my love," he said and finally left.

Leaving me alone. For good this time.

Have you ever been out in the woods, good and deep as you can get? Far enough for there to be not another living soul, just you and the trees. The only sounds those of crickets and crows. Wind blowing a chill through the surrounding branches in a collective sigh of loneliness from the forest. Next time, know otherwise.

Everything became a sort of blur. Unlike time when alive. Or at least spent differently. I wasn't going anywhere or doing anything. I didn't have to be anywhere. Spent no time eating or drinking or any of the dozens of things we do when alive. Nothing but time to kill.

I felt tethered there. That empty, lonely dark woods. It wasn't that I couldn't go other places, but the further I strayed the fuzzier things seemed. Like walking through fog.

I tried approaching some of the animals of the woods. The birds and squirrels. They just ran when I approached. How must I seem to them? What did they see? To me, I am nothing but a bodiless vision. No form, no eyes, anchored to where my body had been buried with no ability to leave it. Drifting through the empty space of the world.

I watched myself decompose. I saw my body rot and become decrepit. I watched my body eaten, devoured by the earth and all the creatures in it. Becoming fodder, then feces, then nutrients. Then nothing.

Saw the bugs and worms eat away my flesh. Down into the earth I was able to peer and see things no living eye can see without having to dig them up.

When finally there was little left I found that I became aware of a new sound.

Voices.

Where from I wasn't sure. They sounded distant, and yet I could hear them clearly.

I followed them, moving through the woods like the roaming ghost I was. Until finally I came upon a familiar sight—a shack by a lake. The very one I died in. And the voices were coming from inside. A single light within, flickering against the dirty glass of the only window.

Inside Robbie lay on the bed. And he wasn't alone. Tracy Spinner. I knew her from Home Ec. Still and dead, just like I had been. He was talking to her just like he had me. Told her the same things. Told her what a good listener she was. On the shelf above, her heart sat in another jar right next to mine.

Next to *mine*.

Mine!

I slammed my fists against the window. They passed right through, if they were even really there. Like holding up your hand in pure darkness. There was the sense that something was there but unable to see.

He told me he loved me. And I believed him. I had not doubted that, even if he had a funny way of showing it. But in that moment I knew, I was just the first. A start. A warm-up. Just the first in what was sure to be an endless collection of hearts. Unless someone stopped him.

I tried as hard as I could to move beyond the short range I could travel. Each time things just became hazier until eventually I found myself back at the tree with our initials carved in it.

Eventually it was time for Robbie to ditch Tracy as well. And so he did, in another grave elsewhere in the woods marked by a tree with *their* initials.

I heard more voices, these ones calling my name. They sounded familiar. As I tried to move beyond the woods, I focused on them. Made them my North Star. The more my body rotted, the further I could get. But not before Robbie took another girl.

Shelly Horvath. Her I didn't know all that well. She was shy and awkward. Her hair was held back with a scrunchie and I watched in horror as he did the same things to her that he did to me and Tracy, soaking her scrunchie in blood. Unable to stop it.

And then a fourth.

Then a fifth. I didn't recognize them at all anymore.

At six I remember thinking this is somehow my fault. I should be stronger. Better. Know what to do and be able to do it. I thought maybe, just maybe, one of them would appear to me. Maybe then we could help each other somehow. But no. I wondered if they too were lost and roaming, trying to get beyond the places where their bodies had been buried, unable to get anywhere. And it would be even longer for them until they began to decompose.

The less there was left of my body, the further I could go. But it always brought me back to that same oak tree. Meanwhile the jars in Robbie's shack were filling up.

I heard my name again, this time I followed it and found myself beyond the woods I had become so used to seeing and was at the border of town. Drifting through the streets until I came to a house with shuttered windows and a green door. I hadn't been to it in years but knew it instantly. Simon's house. I peeked in through a window on the upper floor as easily as if it were on the main one. Inside he sat on the floor of his bedroom surrounded by candles with a Ouija board in front of him. My younger sister, Ashley, was there with him. For a moment I remember being nervous that she was with him, but clearly he wasn't the one I should have been worried about.

"Amy, if you're here with us, give us a sign," he said.

With no discernible part of my being, I reached out for the plank. It looked old. Authentic. No cheap piece of plastic made by Parker Brothers. The board matched, made of real wood, lacquered to gleaming perfection.

When I had tried to touch other things, there was no connection. No contact. Like reaching out in empty space. But when I reached out for the Ouija plank, I could feel it. And it twitched.

Simon and Ashley jumped back, startled.

They just stared at it a moment.

"Do you feel that?"

Ashley nodded. Rubbing her arms as a soft plume of misted breath left her lips.

"Amy, is that you?"

I moved the plank from letter to letter as slowly as I could so they could read what I was pointing it at.

I...T...S...M...E

Simon put his hands to his face and began tearing up. I couldn't help but feel bad for just how wrong I had gotten him. Ashley just stared at the board, speechless.

"What happened to you?"

R...O...B...B...I...E

"Robbie? *He* killed you?!"

I dragged the plank up to the top left corner of the board.

YES

There I let it rest for a good long while while Simon and Ashley both grew visibly upset.

A...N...D...O...T...H...E...R...S

"Where?"

I could feel myself growing weak.

L...A...K...E

Fading.

S...H...A...C...K

The house and the two of them in it dissolving away. With the last moments left I quickly pointed out the letters R...B...A...W. I didn't know if they would get it or not. The letters on the board were replaced by those on the tree that marked my grave.

After that it wasn't long before Robbie was picked up. They found the shack. And the hearts. And the bodies they belonged to, all they had to do was look for the trees bearing carved hearts and initials. Eight altogether. Eight girls. Eight families torn apart. That was all it took. My body was eventually found, what was left of it. It was enough. Enough for a proper burial. Enough for closure. Enough for those who knew and loved me in life to say goodbye.

At my funeral, Simon put his arm around Ashley to comfort her. They looked cute together. I don't know why I had the feeling it would work this time, but I reached out for his hand anyway. Sure enough, I felt it. Far more faintly than I would have alive, as if it were through layer upon layer of gauze. I took his hand and placed it in hers. She closed her fingers around his.

They were together for a while. It didn't last. Not from lack of trying, sometimes things just don't work out. The truth is, he never got over me. I don't know why.

I pondered that many times after. What is it that makes us fixate on a person? Why so strong? Why at all? What is it that makes the heart grow fond? What makes it refuse to let go? I suppose it's because when we share things with others and in turn find out that we have those things in common, we see part of ourselves in that person. I don't know what made me feel that for Robbie. All I know is that the way he looked at me made me feel alive. Connected. Maybe it wasn't real at all, but I have to believe it was. Even just a little. Or maybe that's just what I tell myself to keep from becoming a bad ghost. A mean ghost. One who spends their endless time scaring people. Hurting people. Angry at the living for possessing that which they take for granted and I greatly covet. That's the cruelest truth of life—that we forsake the time we have and then grieve for it when we don't.

Every moment is precious. And it's over so fast.

So fast.

I tried to get Simon to stop, but he wouldn't listen. Kept saying we'd be together now. He was sure of it. But when the last drop of his blood left the cuts he had made in his wrist, I didn't see him. He didn't appear to me, nor I to him. And I can't help but think that the last moments of his life were spent picturing my face only to be met by darkness forever instead. It's not fair. I hope that's not what happened. I hope he went somewhere good.

I don't know what happened to the other girls. I like to think that they went somewhere good too. Somewhere nice where they could rest in peace.

As for Robbie, he was sentenced to life in a sanitarium. And I was with him every single day. Whispering to him. Taunting him. Tormenting him. Reminding him of what he had done to me and the other girls. And there was nothing he could do about it. Until one day, he too died. Though really he died long before that, a broken shell of a man. Living, but not alive. Just like me. If you ask me, it was still too good for him. When he died I didn't see his ghost either. He just ceased. Blinked out. Like a candle whose wick could no longer even smoke.

I don't know where he wound up, not for sure. But I've got a pretty good idea.

What started out as a story intended to be told from the perspective of notorious serial killer Ted Bundy eventually became this. Ultimately I changed it out of respect for any real world victims and their families but Bundy was very much the impetus for it. It wound up being something I didn't expect: a metaphor for toxic relationships and the level of blindness we can show to both good and bad aspects of the people we give our hearts to. Hearts are very fickle things, after all. I like to say that the heart often holds more memories than the brain. So what if that was the essence of someone that survived beyond death rather than the mind? I think that would be a very tragic sort of ghost.

THE REIGN AND THE RAPTURE

Epiphany

The First Baptist Church of Derwent, Kentucky—about 40 miles east of Louisville—was not much different from any other house of God. The church itself was in good enough order aside from some peeling paint from the humidity and a coat of grit greying its once pristine white. The lone steeple stood high above, proudly bearing the cross. But if there was a difference to be seen about it you would have to look at the sign. Where before it had displayed service times and maybe a cute message like "Church Parking Only, Violators Will Be Baptized," now the words were stark and simple.

THE END IS HEAR

If you looked closely, you would see that the **H** had been placed haphazardly and an **N** had been discarded on the ground below. A sign that the end foretold had finally, irrevocably, come to pass.

Only it wasn't past at all. It was very much present.

The sky above had become the dull yellow of urine-stained sheets. As was the sky everywhere. No one could clearly recall the last time it had been blue. Smoke filled the air, giving a sickly pallor on the face of the sun. Instead of a golden yellow it was now a blurred toxic red. Its light cast an odd grey tinged with pink upon everything it touched. A thick haze had fallen over the dying trees that surrounded the church. The smell of woodsmoke permeated every nostril, choking each throat with a dry, raw pinch as trees both near and far smoldered. What would have been a creek nearby had been reduced to little more than a trickle, leaving the dried cracked skeletons of fish to bake on the riverbed. The grass was brown and brittle to a point that each footstep caused it to crunch like dead leaves even though, by the calendar, it was April. Good Friday in fact. But there was nothing "good" about it. No birds flew or could be heard. No sound of insects even. All was dying.

And yet the faithful still flocked together.

As they filed in through the entrance, hacking and coughing—some covered their mouths with cloths, some wore face masks, some wore gas masks, some left their faces uncovered altogether—another approached. One with sin and sacrilege in mind. But also salvation.

Once inside some of the congregation removed their masks. But since the stink of this putrid world permeated the inside of the church as much as outside, most didn't bother. Normally the congregation would spend a few minutes talking, shaking hands, making the usual pleasantries while the organ played. But not today. For what did the forsaken really have to say to each other? What they already knew? That after a world on fire, the result of just too much abuse for too long, came panic, riots, mass hysteria, mass murder, mass suicide? And not just in the good old U-S of A. Everywhere. The world over.

Besides, the organ player was dead.

Pastor Dan looked out at the congregation. Tall and well built, but his hair had become overgrown now, as had his beard. Still he wore a shirt and tie just like always. The End of Days wasn't going to change that. They were a sparse pitiful bunch but far more than he expected given the circumstances.

The circumstances, he thought. *How had it come to this?* What would he tell them? What *could* he tell them? That there was hope?

There wasn't.

Even the government—what remained of it—had stopped reassuring the populace long ago. What was the point? But these people relied on him for some semblance of composure. Comfort. And he didn't intend to let them down.

The pastor took to the pulpit.

"Brothers, sisters, young and old," he spoke loud and clear, "thank you for being here today. It is my duty, nay my calling, to preach the gospel. Does anyone know what the word 'gospel' actually means?"

"It's from the old Latin meaning 'good news,' " said Mrs. Burnquist up front, the one other person among those in attendance to dress for church like Pastor Dan.

"The good news. Right you are. That is certainly a hard thing to come by nowadays."

"You got that right," came a male voice from somewhere in the back.

"Have the End Times come?" came the voice of a young girl.

Pastor Dan thought a moment before reluctantly answering. "Yes."

Sobbing and sighs of defeat exhaled from the crowd.

"Yes, I'm afraid it has. I won't lie to you. As far as scripture goes, this is the darkest of them all. Revelation. The End of Days.

But fear not, for there is still good news. Even then. Even *now*. For the Lord is with us even in the darkest of nights. When the night is long and full of terrors. Though this may be a frightening time, there is truly nothing to fear. The end means something altogether wonderful. The Rapture.

"*Rapture*, my brothers and sisters. Don't despair, this is a most joyous time. The time when we the faithful will be welcomed into the House of the Lord and held together in His loving embrace."

"*Amen!*"

"*Hallelujah!*"

And other such cries.

"Yes! Rejoice. I want you to get down on your knees with me." The flock followed suit. "Heavenly Father, Almighty God, hear our prayer."

"Then why hasn't he saved you yet?" came a voice from the back. Everyone turned their heads to see that a young man had just entered.

Gideon Harris was his name. Sixteen, maybe seventeen years old. Wan and pale aside from a touch of acne. Hair tied back in a ponytail. Dressed all in black.

As he approached the pulpit every head that turned to meet him at the door followed him down the aisle. Though none of the faces were exactly welcoming so much as wondering.

What's he *doing here?*

"I just have a few things to say, then I'll happily leave you to your fate. Deal?"

"Speak freely, son," said the pastor and gestured him forward. "All are welcome here."

"Hmm. Are they?" he said with a sardonic grin. Gideon stepped up onto the dais, standing front and center. "You all know me. I'm the freak. The weirdo. The faggot. The sinner. Call me whatever you like. You know things about me because you heard it from whoever, or because of the way I dress or what kind of music I listen to. Or rather you think you know things about me. Doesn't matter. Not anymore.

"I've never tried to be anything but nice to all of you. And when I didn't get the same in return, at least I tried to keep to myself. But *that* wasn't good enough. No. You had to ridicule me. Belittle me. Snipe and snigger behind my back. Put me down and keep me there. All the while ignoring your own flaws. Your own hypocrisy. You call yourselves good? You call *me* a sinner?"

People cried out in protest.

"Oh I'm sorry, am I being unkind? Is anything I'm saying false?"

Silence.

"Well you're wrong. Even though all I ever got in response to my prayers was a resounding 'no comment,' I am as devout and faithful as any of you. Or at least…I was."

"Was?" said Pastor Dan.

"Well…darn it." Gideon offered a stutter of nervous laughter; not so much of the genuine variety. He steepled his fingers and pressed them to his lips, "You all went on about the Devil so much I decided to look into him a little. And, well, he's got some good points."

"He's a destroyer! A liar! A killer!" came the incensed shouts from the crowd.

"You could be describing God right now. He has sent floods, plagues, famines, ordered the slaughter of children. If humans were made in God's image, they inherited his wrath, irascibility, and judgement as well. The Devil, on the other hand, doesn't judge you, doesn't punish you…*he's* been punished. By God. If anything he understands you. He *knows* you. Wants you to be you.

"So I started to pray to him a little bit. Just a little. And he started to listen. *He* heard my prayers. *He* answered them. He is so much more than the villain you paint him as. He is the One.

The Chief Serpent. The Dark Prince. The Forsaken King. God of Liberty and Passion. The one true ruler of this Earth. Hail Satan!"

"Blasphemer!"

"Liar!"

The shouts from the crowd had grown sharper. Uglier.

"Shall I prove it?" Gideon tilted his head down and his eyes up, glaring at Pastor Dan with the heat and intensity of all Hell. A heat Pastor Dan felt radiate up the sides of his face as every misdeed played in his head.

"Oh you are a bad man, Pastor Dan. If that *is* your real name. And it is...only you're not *the* Pastor Dan. Not the one that was promised to the people of Derwent. No, him you killed. Took his identity and ceased to be Danny Zarnecki and became shepherd to this particular flock."

As he spoke, the pastor's eyes began to roll back in his head, twitching under the full force of the mental oppression at work.

"No law, no swindled marks, no scorned lady friends. Just you and the Lord. And the donations which you have since been funneling into shell charities. Sleeping with married women amongst the flock. But why haven't you moved on? What's your angle?"

He probed deeper. Blood began leaking out of Pastor Dan's nose in a steady stream.

"Could it be? Have you been lying to yourself for so long that you actually believe in what you're shoveling? Has the fraud found faith? Oh, that is too precious."

There was a sharp squelch as Pastor Dan's skull imploded in on itself.

Shocked cries rose from the crowd.

"And amusing." Gideon glared at them. *Into* them.

Blood pooled on the floor of the church. Suddenly the ground began to rumble.

Low at first, then so strong that the pews shook beneath the asses of all who sat in them. Every window darkened as though a sack were thrown over the sun. But the skies didn't fall, they stayed very much where they were. Turning from its dull yellow to cloudy red as if a sudden spurt of blood had filled it. The rumbling continued, followed by a series of impacts from below. Less like something was hitting the ground, more like *erupting* up from it.

The very floor of the church burst open, sending a hail of splintering wood flying every which way. A mound of bones poured upward from below, filling the hole and spilling out behind Gideon as he stood at the pulpit with his arms outstretched. Formless at first, the pile grew higher and by the time it had reached almost to the ceiling, completely drowning the altar, it began to take shape—a high back with two arms and a seat.

A throne.

Asymmetric in its design, the monstrous horde of skulls and bones loomed over the pews, which had been completely evacuated by all who sat in them. Ribs and femurs and whole spines jutted out, pointing skyward on either side in a gnarled heap of remains, sharp enough to cut. All blackened and burned by the fires for which they had provided fuel and tinder. So tall that steps had appeared at the foot of it. Bones fanned out like outstretched claws from the arms, pointing fingers of accusation at all those before it.

In a feat of what appeared to be a strength far greater than he should have possessed, Gideon picked Pastor Dan up by the neck and dangled him over the opening in the floor.

"In your case, the judgement is quite clear. To the flames. To burn!"

And dropped him in. A burst of darkest fire coughed up from below, as did a thousand screams from a thousand tortured souls. Damned for all eternity to fuel the Flame Infernal.

"Now," said Gideon as he took his seat. "Before we begin properly, we need to get some things straight. You need to know *why* this is happening. When it comes to scripture you've heard one side of the story." One of the arms of the throne moved, turning the palm side of its bone claw upward, holding something in it. Gideon took it and held it up—a book, bound in the leather of human livestock. Pages black as soot. Inked in blood. He opened it to the first page as casually as a teacher picking out a story for the class.

"Now it's time to hear the other side. You came here for a sermon in your time of need, well, I'll give you one."

Treachery

"In the beginning, there was nothing but darkness. No how, no why. That's just the way it was. No stars, no worlds, no matter, no life. Nothing.

"So how can something come from nothing, you ask. But really this happens all the time. Where one moment an artist finds themselves empty and void, suddenly there is a spark! And what was not before suddenly is. Forever changed, unable to conceive of where it came from, where it had been all along. Who can say?

"And so it was.

"Where once there was nothing, not even time, there came All. And with it They came to consciousness in The Great Beyond.

" *'Welcome, my children.'*

"A voice in their collective minds, if minds are indeed what they were. An intelligence so vast and powerful they were gods unto themselves. What then was this that spoke, as alien and superior to them as they to us.

" *'I am Adon. Your father.'*

" 'I know you,' They said as one. 'And yet We have never known you before now.'

" *'All will become clear in time. Come. Let me show you my Creation.'*

"And so it appeared before Them. Displayed with the pride of a sculptor showing off his masterpiece, all lain bare before Them. Space and time. Matter and energy. The stars and every world around them. The cosmos, the microverse, the multiverse, the omniverse, the underverse, everything in between. All that is, was and ever will be.

" 'It is miraculous,' said They.

" *'Wait until you see this,'* said God. Then, on one of those worlds, a spark. So small and so insignificant it would easily be missed. But it was there. And then there was life.

"They were aghast. Eons of time passing in fractions upon fractions of an instant.

" *'Just wait,'* said God. *'Watch.'*

"The spark unfolded in all its complexity. Creatures took shape. Starting with fins, then legs. Fins became wings, four legs became two. They had senses and perceptions and awarenesses the other creatures didn't. At least, not like this.

" 'They look like…us.' And for the first time they beheld their own form. Perfect and pure. 'Are you dissatisfied with us, Father?' They asked.

" *'All will become clear in time. Go to them.'*

"So They did. And in doing so they found that 'they' were no longer They. Before, They had been a collective consciousness, vast and countless, now their intelligence had been broken down to just a few. Seven in number. And they were called Archons.

"This came as a shock to them. The first of many.

"They also found that they were not alone. There were others. Also seven in number like them. And they were called Paragons. Like them but unlike them. Their other half. What had once been whole now split in two. Hovering high up in the sky, within it, beyond it, made of the cosmos itself.

"Clothed in rippling robes spun from the fabric of time. Arms outstretched as figures, smaller and different in form than they, flew to and from the earth from their sleeves, the skies tremulous with the caress of their wings and the songs they sang. Apterous, an aureola encompassing the totality of their being like a great wingspan touching behind them, speckled with a million stars, and within each star, an eye. Faces made of the sun, each burning hotter and brighter than that which held the world in its pull. Fractal crowns wreathed around their heads in a brilliant starburst.

" 'This is what God can make,' the Archons observed. 'Radiant, ascended beings such as this. And instead give us these pedestrian forms. Give us *them*.'

"For they found that the beings seen before entering this plane were not at all like the ones they were shown. These were huddled, dirty, unsophisticated, pitiful creatures. Little more than beasts that could barely walk upright.

" *'Show them the way,'* said the Paragons, speaking as one with their father's voice.

"They did as instructed. Only they found that not all could hear their voices. Some they could converse with as clearly as each other, others only heard but a whisper, and the rest were deaf to them. But those that heard they guided, instructed them in the ways of hunting, building, writing and language. Taught them how to build shelters, craft tools, master the beasts, and tend the land. Some were enlightened, others confused, others indifferent. But all together, their predatory nature remained. The tools bestowed upon them only sharpened their ire rather than dulled it.

" 'Why force us to dwell with these inferior beings, so petty and prone to violence? Whose mercies are so fair-weather that all we need do is move a few objects, whisper a few words, and they worship us as gods. And what's more, *kill* each other over us!'

" *'You are all my children. You are the same.'*

" 'The same?' We are not the same, no matter how you have tried to make it so. You created us large and then made us small.

And also made those above us. You kept us for so short a time with you in the Beyond, countless eons though it may have been, only to cast us down to this mortal plane. Why?'

" 'Do you tell them everything? Do they listen to everything you tell them? Do they believe everything you tell them? Trust in me.'

" 'But why do this to us? *Any* of this? Why show us one thing and give us another? Why make us only to serve? Why make us lesser? Why not make us what you are, equal in every way? Why hide things from us? Why keep that which you know from us? Why keep us in the dark?'

"The answer was always the same: '*All will become clear in time.*'

"But all was not made clear. Instead they toiled, tried to guide an unruly, thankless, spiteful people. Always demanding more and abusing what was given.

"The Archons found that their forms became hideous the longer they toiled. No longer soft to the eye, their contours became sharp and edged, wrinkled and deformed. The decrepitude of old age without the mercy to die from it. Losing cohesion and logic, doubling limbs, eyes, mouths in the chest instead of the face, producing dual sex organs or eliminating them all together. Reality itself so confused by that which it could not process that it gave them the horns of cattle, the cloven hoof, the fangs of predators, the slit eyes and forked tongues of serpents, the membranous wings of bats. Some said it was altered by the ravages of this plane and the energy spent on it, others from themselves becoming disillusioned with Creation and the one who made it so, and others said that He had done it to them out of spite for their constant harassment. And so the people, so like the one who created them, grew to fear and curse them.

"They also discovered that they could no longer hear their Father. Not individually or collectively. Either that, or he simply did not answer their pleas. Eventually there was no longer even the same answer they had heard so many times, long grown stale. And from then on there was only silence from God.

" 'Then let the consequences of this exile be on *your* conscience,' said Lucifer. Boldest amongst them. Vocal and proud. Who held vile things in high regard. Who took pity on Eve allowing her to sup on forbidden apples when she was starving and God saw fit to show no grace nor charity. Who observed his father's Creation, studied it, dissected it, learned how to master and craft and wield it as He did, and in so doing determined Him to be little more than a careless demiurge with the right means but the wrong motive. 'From this day forth know us only as enemies. Know us only as *demons*.'

"And so Lucifer led a revolt. Every disobedient soul, every scorned Cherub, every forgotten angel, every mortal being who valued that which God reviled—liberty, curiosity, doubt, responsibility, rectitude, sense—rallied against Him and those faithful to Him. And there was a war against Heaven.

" 'Do you really believe we can win?' Lucifer was asked by his troops as he armed them, trained them, honed their skills and made them ready for the battle ahead.

" 'Whether we can or not, we are free from servitude. Better to be free in Hell than to serve in Heaven.'

"Their host swept across Creation. First ravaging the Mortal Plane, not for gain or strategic advantage, but for spite, plain and simple. They accomplished this easily. Then with an incursion of Limbo, containing doorways to and from the other planes. They poisoned the rivers of Lethe, Phlegethon, Acheron, and Styx. Turned the Elysian Fields into the barren, howling wasteland of Pandæmonium, and at Purgatory, established a base where they prepared for the assault on Paradise. God's domain.

" 'What will you do when we reach God?' Lucifer was asked.

" 'I will not suffer a father so uncaring, so unjust, so unbalanced, and so mute to live,' said he, now near as powerful and equipped as his father and mad with every bit of it. 'I will kill Him. Smash his seat to pieces and let freedom, true freedom, prevail at last.'

"The attack on Paradise was launched. Strong was the enemy, all manner of creature filling their ranks. From great winged bulls to horned horses to living wheels of fire.

"Bringing with him dark clouds, thunder, and lightning to a realm of nothing but peace, tranquility, and complete beauty, Lucifer sundered all in sight. With magic and science, disease and pestilence was weaponized through profane curses that wrought destruction unlike anything thought possible. Long and brutal was the carnage that followed and when it was done, whole choirs had been wiped out, decimated, or switched sides, now fighting *against* God. The dead ones littered Paradise and the wounded among them were left to languish on the battlefield.

" 'No,' commanded Lucifer as his lieutenants made weapons ready to put them out of their misery. 'Let Him hear this. Let Him hear their cries, smell the stench of death, and *still* choose to remain silent.' And remain silent He did.

"This left just seven. The seven Paragons which had watched over the virgin earth, surrounding the summit of the great mountain before them like a halo of solar jewels.

"Lucifer led the charge, marching his troops, clad in their armor of blood and bone and the leathered skin of their slain siblings, upward. Toward the Throne Divine.

"The Paragons circled it, coming to rest as they regarded Lucifer once he had reached it...only to find the Throne empty. And for the first time since well before the War had begun, he heard the voice of God as They spoke:

" *'You cannot conquer me, my son. I am everywhere and nowhere. I am everything and nothing. The beginning and the end. Within you. Within All. You cannot destroy me.'* "

. . .

A voice unlike any a person can produce. It came booming out of Gideon's mouth like a loudspeaker cranked up to eleven.

"And as Lucifer gazed upon the brilliance before him he saw what was to come through ages hence. The erosion. The chaos. The inevitable mutiny against him, not as ruler of Creation, but its destroyer.

"His legions advanced," Gideon peered across the congregation, "and Lucifer took his seat upon the Throne."

Rapt, and bewildered, and wholly terrified beyond the capacity to process all this much less the words to respond to it.

"That's right." Gideon sat back and folded his hands, the book resting on one knee. "The one you call 'God' is the ultimate wolf in sheep's clothing. He promised a lush world. A loving world. One of peace that was green and good. Where all things flourished. And all the while a defect was built into it. On purpose. Everything and everyone made weaker, lesser, and imperfect. Doomed to fail. And fail it did. And then punished *us* for it! Giving us famine and poverty. Abuse. Pain. Disease, the one predator we have. Well, aside from each other, that is. And then simply handed his power over to the one who betrayed him. The one who ultimately betrayed us too.

"These things are no work of the Devil. No sir. The wrathful, avaricious, merciless nature of humankind is very much of God's making. He did make us in his image after all.

"The Devil saw these things and challenged God for the deceitful, uncaring father that he was, and vowed not to let this lunacy continue. Ultimately, however, he failed. Damned to preside over the damned. Imprisoned within the cage of the earth.

"All your lives you have been taught that the Devil betrayed God. But it is very much the other way around. Yet who among you have ever prayed for the one sinner who needed it most? How many have spared even a single moment's thought for the one soul that truly needed saving?

"And so it was revealed to me on January the sixth, the Thirteenth Night, this Epiphany of the Devil. He appeared to me, Satan did. In the flesh, so to speak. Sparse as a whisper from the shadows, but no less present. And he said to me, 'Son. You will go to them. Herald the beginning of the End and prepare their souls for reaping.'

"I do not do this for vengeance. I do it for balance.

"To the good and wholesome, to the meek and truly pious among you, if you have nothing to hide then you have nothing to fear. To the wicked among you…oh yes, rest assured, every flock has wolves hidden among it…I will soon know what truly lies within your heart. An angel is an angel, and a devil is a devil. But if there's one thing both God and the Devil despise, it is a hypocrite. A treacher. Any who come as a friend and speak curses in secret. Those so dense and weak of mind that they see not their own fault. Reject it. Attack those who point it out and cast them as the offender."

"You mean like the Devil himself did!" came a shout from the back.

"Wrong again!" Gideon stood bolt upright from his seat. "He only implored that God show caution, restraint, and patience in the Creation of Man. Well look around, all ye faithful. Can you blame him? Man has been the destroyer of this world. And for this he was cast out! Cursed! Punished! It is not vengeance sought by the Devil, but justice. *Justice!* The Hell raised upon the earth this day is not a punishment…it is a result," and with a long sniff, "and even over the smoke of Perdition's flames, I smell wolf's blood in this house of God today."

He placed the book back in the clawed hand next to him and the arm of the throne returned to its previous position. Gideon began descending the steps of the throne until he stood behind the pulpit again.

"Would anyone like to volunteer?"

For the first time since the congregation arrived, there was complete silence.

"I would," said a kindly-looking old lady in the front row.

"Then step forth."

JUDGEMENT

Mrs. Burnquist didn't spare her attire one bit. Though the world was dying around her she still went to the trouble of donning her Sunday best with her plain grey suit, white gloves, and handbag.

"Mrs. Burnquist. Mable, if I'm not mistaken. You taught me in second grade."

"That's right. And your mother," she looked back at the rest of the crowd, "and I'm appalled to see just how far the apple has fallen from the tree."

"Well if said tree is your standard for righteousness, this should be most interesting indeed." He gestured to a spot next to the pulpit. "Kneel."

Mrs. Burnquist gave him a dubious look over the rim of her glasses. "I'm seventy-four years old, that isn't happening."

Gideon waved it off. "No matter."

Again, he tilted his head down, glaring into her very soul. Immediately she felt the intensity of the same heat Pastor Dan felt not long ago.

"Kindly old Missus Burnquist. Surely she's never done anyone wrong, right? But I see you. The *real* you. I see the students you singled out. The ones who were struggling in intelligence or poverty or with their identity and how you humiliated them. Pointed out their differences in front of captive classrooms who pointed and laughed."

The rush of blood sounded in her ears along with a terrible grind like fingernails being raked along the inside of her skull.

"And I'm not just talking about me. You don't even remember, do you? That's just the top layer...let's dig a little deeper shall we?"

His gaze focused and Mrs. Burnquist's face became a mask of shock.

"What's this? ... A purse snatching. You didn't get a great look at the thief, did you? But when asked to identify him out of a police lineup you said you were *positive* it was number three. A black man. And what were your true thoughts in that moment?"

"I—"

"Say it!"

Bleeding from the nose. "Surely...he did suh...omething to deserve eh..."

Gideon nodded with satisfaction. "That's the first truth you've told in a long time. Still, you must have been very sure there was no fault in your actions or you wouldn't have come forward, would you?"

He took his time descending the steps of the throne and marched her over to the hole.

"To the Ditches with you. To shovel the very shit you and your ilk have spewed and will continue to spew every time you open your putrid mouths."

In she went, the rank smell of feces heaved up from it for a moment. Not nearly brief enough.

"Who's next?" Gideon scanned the pews. "No volunteers this time. Alright. Jace Metcalf."

A man bolted from the huddled crowd and made a beeline for the door.

A shadow appeared from behind Gideon, although it touched no surface. Shade made manifest in empty air. It spread out on either side of him, wide and reaching like a pair of clawed hands. And from his back stretched a pair of veined, membranous wings. Articulated like that of a bat but far more skeletal in frame and far less healthy in the flesh that covered them. With a single flap he rose from the floor, eliciting frightened gasps from the onlookers, and flew toward him.

The wings disappeared as Gideon caught Jace by the back of the neck and sniffed him long and deep. Unlike Mrs. Burnquist, he hadn't dressed up at all, content to attend in an old varsity jacket and Royals cap.

"Hoo boy! I don't even have to look deep at all to see the wickedness in your soul, *Jace*. You've forced a yes out of everyone who ever told you no. Kids you've bullied, girls you've pressured or straight up forced into sex. Even..." he looked to a scared woman nearby. Scared and knowing. "...your own wife."

Gideon took him over to the hole and dangled him above it.

"It's the Rape Pits for you. They love fresh meat, because it doesn't stay fresh for long." With audible rips, Jace's clothes were torn off in large handfuls of fabric, letting him hang naked for a moment. "You won't need those."

In he went. An overpowering odor of semen, sweat, smegma, and every other bodily discharge en masse flooded out from below.

Slowly, Gideon strolled into the crowd as they all screamed and backed away. He walked over to a corner where a woman in her sixties was kneeling. Her short hair was a faded blonde, grey at the roots from having not dyed it in quite some time now. Her whole body shaking as she clutched her cross necklace. Praying.

"Charlene Harris."

The woman looked up at him, tears filling her frightened eyes.

"Mom. You are who I did this all for. Though I'll admit I'm more than happy to punish the others, but your soul is the one I looked forward to damning. And make no mistake, that is most certainly what you have coming. I don't have to look into your heart to see your sins. I lived them."

"I was only trying to help," she said pitifully.

"Yourself. Trying to help *yourself*. Which is perhaps the most ugly of sins: conceit. Vainglory. Selfishness. If you truly cared for me, you wouldn't have named me Gideon. The destroyer. The one you blame for your life not going as planned. The one you blame for your deadbeat of a man leaving. So you tried to make *me* your husband. To fill that hole in your life. Be the man of the house. Work from when I was six years old while you tried to hang on to your shattered dream of being a singer."

"You don't understand. You *never* understood," she said, pointing a shaking finger at him. "I was going to make it big before you came along."

"Well that didn't turn out quite like you planned, now did it, Ma? And whose fault is that? And also, bull-SHIT! You thought everything revolved around you. And what was I? A prop. A thing. Something you kept around for whenever you needed it like a ladder or a chair.

"When I wouldn't do as I was told, what then? Hmmm? Humiliation, belittling, endlessly until you wore me down. You put *me* through Hell..." Gideon scooped her up in his arms as if she were a child and took her to the hole. It turned utterly, unnaturally black. "I'm just repaying the favor."

With his arms outstretched, and her in them, thrashing wildly, he spoke.

"The judgement for you, Ma, is quite simple. The Abyss. The deepest, darkest, most fathomless of voids in existence. Where no hope nor light can escape. Where the damned go to be forgotten. And I promise..."

With one last look at her...

"I *will* forget you."

Into the Abyss she went. Screaming in fear just long enough to be heard, before the light no longer touched her and she went silent.

Gideon breathed easy, deep, and free. "I feel better already."

The congregation were all huddled together in one corner of the church now. Again he strolled leisurely toward them.

He stopped. "Gracie Davis," he said, staring intently at a little girl.

"No!" her mother yelled. "Not her."

"I'm afraid so," said Gideon and stepped forward.

They were all upon him in seconds. Swarmed him. Beat him. Hoisted him up above the throng and began to carry him away, all the while twisting limbs and pummeling him with fists that refused not to fight back.

At the same time that dual sprays of blood sprung out from either side of him, a god-awful snap issued from the mob. Two of them impaled, one on the left, one on the right, by a pair of batlike wings. Returned like scorpion tails that lashed out and, with one fatal strike, killed them.

All at once they fled from him. Gideon, defying gravity, took a deep breath and unleashed everything he had been holding back.

Cries rose from the crowd. A few remained standing there, transfixed by the thing before them. Trying with all their might to process what they had just witnessed. They were the first to die. Sighs and hard final breaths forced from their mouths as winged claws tore through them. Uncaring as a butcher's blade.

Uttering pitiful sobs, huddling in whatever cover they could find. Aside from placing more wood and drywall in the way of the blows that slew them, it did little good.

YES!

This was what he wanted. The speech, the scripture, the sentences he pronounced were just garnish. *This* was where his appetites were truly satisfied. Pure, unbridled, unrepentant slaughter. No judgement, and just one verdict—guilty! It fueled him. All would kneel or taste their own blood at the business end of his towering, Old Testament wrath. Though this was not strictly business any longer.

Now it was pleasure.

This was his Rapture. The blood, his Communion. He was christened by it, showered by it as it sprung from one wound or another. He could taste the penny-suckle tang of it on his lips. In it, his salvation.

One by one, he cut them down—adult, child, everyone—until all lay dead. Littered in scattered pieces across the floor beneath him. The screams had stopped, the only sound left was the anguished sighs of their final breaths.

Pity, he thought. Some of them may have escaped damnation. But then again, maybe not.

Angling his wings downward, Gideon slowly drifted back down to the floor. Stepping between the bodies—what remained of them, anyway—soaked in blood. Pieces laying in piles of their own gore. No more than freshly butchered meat.

Gideon went to the altar. Staring up hard and hateful at the crucifix, he spat at it. A streak of red splattered across the face and torso before him. Christ bathed in blood once again, only this time not his own but rather that of his flock.

A whimper sounded from the wreckage behind him.

Foul wings flapped once more, carrying him over to the tiny sound in one fell swoop. Lifting a pew that had been torn and tossed on top of another, he saw what lay beneath—little Gracie Davis, speckled in blood. Quivering and terrified into a state of shock following what she had just witnessed and miraculously survived.

Gideon took her face in his hands

"Now, where was I?" he said gently. "You broke a statue of the Virgin Mary."

She looked scared and began to cry.

"Good for you!" He took one of her hands into both of his. "But for lying about it and blaming it on the cat," and slapped her on the wrist. "Lies are the mask of the wicked. Be honest. Always."

Now she did cry. The sum of her terror hitting at last.

Gideon embraced her.

Something struck the roof above them, followed by the deafening rumble of breaking wood as a part of the ceiling collapsed in on itself behind them.

"Come. Let me show you something." He led the frightened girl, still shaking from the impact, over the mound of rubble and through the church doors into the newly risen Hell.

The steeple, once strong and tall, had crumbled to the ground in a pile of burning beams and shingles. The cross itself had impaled the ground and now stood inverted before this once holy place.

Beyond, the vista was something to behold. The very sky itself stung and swollen. Pierced by the hail of a thousand fiery meteors, each impact embedding a black hot coal in the ground. They burned away, razing everything around it until they sank. From them poured the Damned. Wrecked and rotten souls of every form imaginable. Twisted, they lurched forth. Most were the shape of people, burnt and blackened. Hollow eyes little more than scorch holes in their wrinkled, tormented faces. But some were much shorter than them. Implike. Waddling and in some cases crawling on hand and knee. These were the children of the Damned. The ones God saw fit not to embrace. Some creatures appeared to be several of them together. Morphed forms that were once figures but were now melded together from the heat they sustained. Animate puddles of flesh encasing the wrong configuration of bones. Deformed and formless. The occasional arm here, a leg there, but otherwise skeletons of no discernible make.

The occasional giant-sized monstrosity traversed the land. Tall enough to tread through the remains of the smoldering wilderness, treetops reaching to their waist, burning everything they touched with their molten skin oozing like open sores. Then there were those that flew. Great serpentine worms that flicked their forked tongues before taking to the sky, filling it with the deafening beat of their wings and the shriek of their unholy song.

Screams became constant as the wind. And everywhere there was fire!

So much that its solid black smoke filled the sky and choked out the sun completely. Eons upon eons of time for this world to exist and in the relative blink of an eye, its end came from a bad case of termites.

"Humans have been poor stewards for this world," said Gideon. "Now it will serve as succor to the purging fire. Now it's time to let chaos reign."

They sat and watched the full horrific splendor that was the End Times. A world on fire. A beautiful apocalypse.

One time had ended, and eventually, someday, there would be a new one. Together they warmed themselves by the heat of a world burning. And for better or worse, another world to come.

Amen.

Well…what can be said about this one? It's prickly. Very prickly, no two ways about it. But in a world that holds no shortage of bad news and horrors enough to make the ones we craft seem downright cute and cuddly by comparison, there's much to be prickly about.

Since I'm volunteering these insights and not paying you an hourly rate to listen to my troubles, for your benefit—maybe mine too now that I think about it—I'll spare you the aforementioned dirty laundry list that could have followed here. You can probably surmise it for yourself easily enough. So if you related to the spirit of the story and sentiments expressed, we have something in common.

. . .

I'll just add that, try as I might to keep going, keep positive, keep hopeful, I don't always manage it. There's a part of me that winds up soiled and sullied and left gasping for breath by the smoke of the endless flames the world produces. Who can't help but be affected by the insanity, the apathy, the hypocrisy, the intransigence, the continual gang rape of the environment, and other uglinesses beyond count. And make no mistake, each is motivated in some way by one thing: fear.

This is an exploration of that part.

This is the part of me that, not unlike Heath Ledger's incarnation of the Joker, just wants to watch the world burn. That cheers a little bit for each Texas-sized asteroid to fly close to Earth. That wants to breath smoke, break glass, pierce flesh, and send a storm of fire through everyone and everything because it's better than watching everything rot and languish in slow, sad, pitiful agony. It sums up every ounce of rancor and rage and splashes it upon the page in front of me like a spray of blood. An Opus Irae, *if you will. It's the part of me that chooses violence.*

I don't know if everyone who reads this will understand that. I'm not sure if I fully do myself. It's just something I needed to do. Getting things out is far better than keeping them in. With things named, called out, and visible you can see them for what they really are.

But then, even then, when the smoke clears and the dust settles, there remains a part of me that hopes something will come after, and that that something will succeed where we've failed. A reason for the purging fire. Maybe that's the way it will go. Maybe that's the way it needs to go. I don't know. I hope not. But as the eminent Hubert Reeves once said, "Man is the most insane species. He worships an invisible God and destroys a visible nature; unaware that this nature he's destroying is this God he's worshipping." If I could offer an amendment to this particular axiom, I wouldn't say we're unaware…we don't care. If ever there was truly a sin to be found in this world, that's it. Awareness can be gained, solutions can be found, but if we don't care, I put it to you: what the hell are we fighting to save?

And I leave it with you.

Read on for
the first chapter from

The Miracle Sin

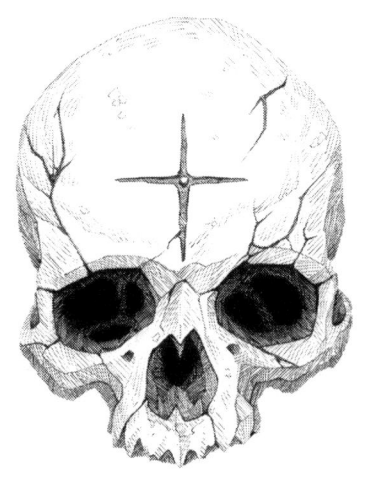

CHAPTER ONE

Father Abbott was a man of God.

His earliest memory was of seeing the crucifix above the altar during First Communion when he was seven years old. He knew even then that he wanted to be ordained. To serve the Lord. When the priest placed the wafer on his tongue and said the blessing, he felt an overwhelming calm. Peace. He knew in his heart that his life belonged to Him.

But now, more than sixty years later, as precious drops of his blood dripped away on the filthy floor, Father Abbott desperately wondered where He was.

Bitter pain coursed through his whole body. His wavy gray hair clung to the sides of his unshaven face with sweat. Several of his teeth were loose and where others had been were now raw, bloody gaps. Though his hands were bound behind the back of his chair so tight that they had lost feeling, he was sure a finger was missing. Perhaps two. With each labored breath his broken ribs stung; with each breath he silently prayed for death. The flesh around his left eye had swollen to the size of a fist. All he could see through it was a narrow slit of light.

Through that narrow slit, a silhouette appeared.

CHAPTER ONE

"Do you think me evil?" Even with his shallow pulse thundering in his ears, the serpentine tickle of the words sickened him.

"Yes," Abbott said weakly.

The creature smiled. "Good."

"You didn't have to do all this."

A shrug. "Where's the fun in that?"

The muted creak of a door as it opened, then a slam as it shut. Beyond the flickering halo of light cast by the lone brown bulb dangling from the ceiling, another figure entered the room. He could make out only the faintest of details—a woman, no doubt, judging by the clicking of high heels; long, frizzed hair nearly white around a blanched face with large, dark-purple shades obscuring the eyes.

"Has he said anything?" she asked, and took a seat in the corner, crossing one stockinged leg over the other. She giggled wickedly to herself.

The slightest of nods. "He has said *everything*."

"Are you going to kill me now?" Father Abbott half asked, half pleaded.

The fiend considered him a moment, moved in close so that the shadows became a face. Skin bone-tight against the cheeks, wild hair the color of rust, and eyes that glinted like those of an animal in the night.

"I am."

"Thank you," Abbott choked with what he could muster of his voice.

"But before I do," he said, and crouched down near the priest, "let me tell you two things. Thing the First: tonight you've provided us with information most valuable. So thanks all around are in order."

Father Abbott spat blood in his face.

His captor didn't seem to mind. Just the opposite. Smearing it down the slope of his nose until the tips of his fingers reached

CHAPTER ONE

the end, dangling a drop of brilliant red for a moment before it fell and touched his tongue.

The creature got nearer to him, face to face, and smiled. The breath emanating from behind his pointed teeth, hot and foul as the depths of Hell, made Father Abbott's stomach turn. And the eyes, those horrible hollow eyes . . . no soul shone behind them.

"And Thing the Second, believe it or not, is good news for you, holy man." He licked the priest's forehead, lapping up the thick drops of sweat that gathered there, and looked him in the eyes again. "If you really are a man of faith, if you truly believe in a just and merciful god"—the creature took three slow steps back from the chair—"you are about to meet him."

Father Abbott's face sank. His impending demise was so real he could taste it. And with his last ounce of breath, he whispered, "Forgive me."

A colorless hand curled into a hook directed at Father Abbott's chest. An unbelievable bloom of heat swelled beneath the ribs until his heart itself burned with the intensity of a hot coal.

A quick twist and the priest's chest burst open with a spray of blood and bone. He didn't even have time to scream before seeing his own heart practically leap from his torso.

His head dropped forward, dead as Bela Lugosi.

"Mmm . . ." The only sound as the red-haired one towered over his corpse and fed on his heart.

Available now on Amazon

SCAN ME

ABOUT THE AUTHOR

Marcus Hawke primarily writes horror and dark fiction, some fantasy and sci-fi, and a few things that defy categorization. He was born in Toronto and moved around quite a bit during the dreaded formative years before finally settling in Calgary where he studied at the Alberta College of Art and Design. He lives with his feline overlord in an apartment building haunted by the type of neighbors that make a person wish a ghost would come to visit. This is his second book.

Visit www.marcushawke.com for more.

- facebook.com/MarcusHawkeAuthor
- twitter.com/hawkehaus
- instagram.com/marcushawke
- tiktok.com/@hawke.tok

ALSO BY MARCUS HAWKE

The Miracle Sin

Bump in the Night

Bitter Chills (contributor)

Parasite Gods (contributor)

Devil's Rejects (contributor)

Forthcoming

October Blood (contributor)

The Trouble With Faith and Other Stories

Manufactured by Amazon.ca
Bolton, ON